Julie Bozza

Of Dreams
and Ceremonies

LIBRAtiger

Published by LIBRAtiger 2018

ISBN: 978-1-925869-21-7

First published by Manifold Press 2013

libra-tiger.com | juliebozza.com

Acknowledgements

Once more, I am humbly hoping for the reader's tolerance. Part of this story deals with things that some will say don't concern me. But, as before, I do so with nothing in my heart but a love of and a wish for interdependence between all our peoples – and for that perhaps any infelicities will be forgiven.

wedding

one

Dave slept late that first morning, and when he woke he was alone. Nicholas's bedroom loomed large and empty around him. It was on one corner of the house, so there were two big windows on each of two walls, and the curtains were hanging wide open – which was apparently Nicholas's habit – so the place seemed full of light and air. The room contained an odd collection of furniture, some of it apparently very old, but all of it comfortable. Almost everything that wasn't wood was blue – upholstery, carpet, curtains, ornaments and oddments. And then there were books, a whole heap of books scattered everywhere.

There was also an en suite bathroom, thank God, which he promptly made use of, but then Dave headed back to the four-poster bed. He didn't get in again, but hefted up to sit on the side of it with his feet hanging some distance off the floor, and he looked around him quietly, still a bit dazed with jet lag. Well, with jet lag and with the enormity of what he'd done.

He, David Taylor of Brisbane, Australia – a quite ordinary bloke who'd spent almost all his conscious life in love with his best friend Denise and assuming he was straight – had fallen in love with Nicholas Goring, the youngest son of an English earl, while acting as his tour guide during a seven-week journey in Australia's Outback. Yesterday evening, having flown halfway round the world to belatedly follow Nicholas to his home in Buckinghamshire, Dave had even agreed to marry the man.

"Well," Nicholas had explained a little later, once his dauntingly large family had finally quit congratulating them, "it's a civil partnership, not a marriage. It's a civil partnership ceremony, not a wedding."

Which all sounded like far too many tongue-fumbling syllables for Dave. "How do you think about it?" he'd asked.

Nicholas had grinned so wide and so happy it was almost impossible to believe that one person could feel so ecstatic. "I'm getting married!"

"Good," said Dave. "Then that's what it is."

Now that he was alone in Nicholas's natural habitat, Dave took the opportunity to consider his surroundings. Though the room was full, it didn't seem cluttered so much as well lived in. There was the bed, of course, a free-standing wardrobe, and three assorted armchairs loosely arranged around a low coffee table. There was a serious-looking desk with a laptop computer and a scatter of papers, magazines and the like. Beside it, a bookcase reached towards the high ceiling, full to overflowing with books. The books were really the only thing that didn't fit in with the blue colour scheme, and so they made random rainbows along the shelves, in a couple of piles on the desk and the table, and in a smaller stack on Nicholas's bedside set of drawers. A couple of paintings on the wall were of landscapes and therefore introduced some green into the room, though really they were mostly sky. There was also a glass case on a side table, containing the pinned remains of various butterflies – at which Dave didn't look too closely.

A large chest of drawers stood by the bathroom door with a tall mirror beside it. Dave leaned a little to the right so he could peer at himself, wondering if he looked as vague as he felt. Yes, he did. It was the different time zones, maybe. Despite his long night's sleep, he thought that maybe his body was still on Australian time – and no doubt as far as his body was concerned it was still the middle of the night.

As Dave sat back up again he noticed four framed photos standing on top of the chest of drawers, and he went over to investigate. There was one of what must be Nicholas's parents – a much younger Richard than the man Dave had met the previous day, formally posed beside a rather smart-looking woman with Nicholas's dark hair and pale skin, his long face and unusual beauty. Another photo was a far more informal close-up of Nicholas and his nephew Robin, all hugs and laughter.

The other two photos had been taken in Australia, at the remote waterhole where Nicholas had discovered a new species of butterfly. The photo of Nicholas was one that Dave himself had taken – the first of their butterflies had alighted on Nicholas's Akubra, and there was a wickedly joyous look on the face peeking up from under the brim. The photo of Dave was one he hadn't even been aware of Nicholas taking. In it, Dave was sitting back reading one of his Patrick O'Brian books, lost in the long-ago maritime world. Another of the blue butterflies had settled on his shoulder, and seemed to also be contemplating the novel.

Near the framed photos was a glass cube in which one of the blue butterflies had been preserved. Dave considered it, remembering.

He and Nicholas had spent three weeks as friends, and four weeks as lovers. It wasn't much, perhaps, on which to base a marriage, but once Dave had gotten past his initial resistance, there had been a certainty about the relationship. Though he hadn't admitted it to himself at the time, even his resistance had felt as if he were fighting the inevitable. So it hadn't taken very much to push him into finally following Nicholas back home to England. Maybe it was just the way that Dave did these things: after all, he and Denise had been inseparable since the day they'd first met. Maybe Dave was just an all–or–nothing kind of guy.

Dave sighed, and reflected that it was time for a cup of tea – or coffee if he could get it. Wherever Nicholas had gone, it seemed he wasn't coming back soon, and it was eleven–thirty already. Dave had a quick shower in the en suite, and pulled on a clean t–shirt and pair of jeans. He was probably hopelessly under–dressed for an English manor house, but his self–imposed budget had only allowed for a couple of new nicer items, and he thought he'd better save them for best.

It was only as he collected his watch from the low table on his side of the bed that he realised Nicholas had left him a note.

Good morning, David – or good afternoon! Take your time, and come down when you're ready. Simon will keep an eye out for you, and I'll be somewhere around. Try the conservatory?

Nicholas x

There was an arrow pointing to the kiss, and a promise: *To be delivered in person ASAP.*

Dave grinned, took a breath, and headed out of the sanctuary of Nicholas's bedroom.

As Dave walked down the main staircase into the hall, Simon – the family butler – did indeed put his head out of a door concealed in the wood panelling, and then came out to offer a smile and a good morning. "I hope you slept well, Mr Taylor," he added without even a hint of innuendo, when Dave was all too conscious that everyone must be assuming he and Nicholas spent a fair amount of time and effort the previous night in … getting reacquainted. And their assumptions would be right, too.

"I slept very well, thank you, Simon."

"I'm glad to hear it –" After a moment's pause he finished with "David" rather than Mr Taylor.

"Actually, I know I said David yesterday, but is there any chance of you calling me Dave? You're probably the only person here who will."

"Dave, then," Simon obligingly agreed. "You're probably in need of tea or coffee, and perhaps a late breakfast of some kind?"

"Please, yeah, coffee would be great. And something to eat – though I guess it's almost lunchtime?"

"Come this way, Dave, and I'll show you the family kitchen. You can make your own drinks there at any time. Mrs Gilchrist – our cook and housekeeper – will be serving lunch to the family at one, but of course we'll make sure you have something to tide you over until then."

They'd gone through the concealed door, past an office which Dave thought must be Simon's, and then headed down a very plain staircase to the basement level, where they proceeded along an unadorned corridor. Dave had watched enough British TV to realise that this must be the servants' domain.

"Thanks," Dave said, following along. "I have to say, I am kind of hungry." It was the long sleep and irregular hours, he thought. Never mind the exercise he'd had both yesterday afternoon soon after he'd arrived and last night as well, all in the cause of getting reacquainted. At this point he needed sustenance just to cope.

The family kitchen turned out to be a room off the main kitchen – perhaps it was an old walk–in pantry or storage room converted – with a water cooler, an urn and a fridge, work benches and cupboards, and a high table with stools. Simon gave him a quick tour. "There will always be supplies here for you to make a hot drink and a sandwich, whenever you have need. And we tend not to serve formal lunches if it's just the family. By which I mean the family who live here."

"I get it," said Dave, his attention more on the sandwich Simon was making for him, and his hands wrapped warm around the mug of coffee Dave himself had already made while Simon was showing him round. "Thank you." He was rather relieved to know he'd be expected to fend for himself at some stage during an ordinary day.

Mrs Gilchrist came through from the main kitchen for a moment to be properly introduced; Dave stood and shook her hand before she headed back into the bustle.

"With everyone here," Simon explained, "that's twenty family members to cater for. Twenty–one now," he added with a nod towards Dave. "You'll understand if we're a bit stretched."

"Yeah," Dave said with a wry half–grin, in between bites of the sandwich. "Should have known it would be bad timing."

"On the contrary, it's excellent timing. Everyone is glad of the opportunity to meet you." Simon lowered his voice to confide, "The family are very happy that you came, you know. We all are."

"Thanks," he replied, hoping he had even a small chance of measuring up to whatever these people expected of him.

Simon tactfully changed the subject. "On most days I'm sure you'll be glad to know it's a great deal quieter than this! Nicholas and his father Lord Goring live here, along with Nicholas's oldest brother Robert and his family – his wife Penelope, and their children Robin and Isabelle."

That made him grin properly. "I actually have faces for all those names already."

"Well done," Simon said with a smile that bore not the faintest hint of irony or condescension. "You'll be fine, Dave. There's not a person here who doesn't welcome you."

Dave couldn't help but wonder how that could be. His scepticism must have been plain to read.

"Everyone adores Nicholas, and it's been rather obvious since his return from Australia that you're what makes him happiest."

Dave coloured up, and muttered something about Nicholas having found the butterflies.

"Yes, sir – but he also found you."

Two mugs of coffee, a sandwich and an apple later, Dave was feeling rather more human. "I'm sure you have things you're busy with," he said to Simon. "I shouldn't keep you."

"That's perfectly all right, Dave. I'll take you to Nicholas, shall I? I believe he's in the garden."

"He said something about the conservatory."

"Ah, he and Robin were finished in there by about ten–thirty."

"Right! Garden it is."

Simon led him down another corridor, and then up a narrow staircase to reach a cloakroom at the back of the house – which contained an extraordinary collection of different gum boots, a row of coats, and a laundry–style sink. From there, a door opened onto a large paved area. The basement had been rather a warren, but Dave's sense of direction hadn't quite failed him yet.

"I think you'll find that Nicholas is talking with Frank, who helps tend the garden," Simon said as he ushered Dave out onto the terrace. "He used to be the chauffeur, and he still maintains the cars, but he no longer drives."

"Ah," said Dave. The infamous chauffeur. Nicholas's first love. "Did he get too old to drive? Lose his licence?"

"No, sir. There was an accident. Nothing of any real account, but there was nerve trauma which affected his vision. He felt it best if he gave it up. A matter of safety for himself and the family."

"I thought – Nicholas spoke of him as having retired."

"Well, I suppose that's how we all considered it, in many ways, though it wasn't due to age." The two of them were strolling along the terrace very slowly now. Simon cast Dave a discreetly querying look.

Dave nodded. It was perfectly obvious what wasn't being said. "Nicholas told me about … how he felt for the man. Frank."

"Frank Brambell."

"Right. But I thought it was meant to be a big secret. Nicholas didn't tell me much – not even Frank's name. Didn't want to embarrass anyone. Does he know that you know?"

"I shouldn't think so."

The two of them came to a halt, and Dave considered Simon for a long moment. "You know pretty much everything that goes on around here, don't you?"

"You've nothing to fear from me on that account, Mr Taylor."

"No, of course not. I just meant – Well, can I talk to you? Sometime soon. I need to ask you about something. Nothing to do with Frank."

"Of course. Shall we say eleven tomorrow morning? I usually have a quiet hour or so before lunch."

"Perfect. Thanks." Dave added, "You really don't have to call me Mr Taylor, you know."

"Habit, sir, I'm sorry – long ingrained!" Simon led them off again, and they headed down some steps onto a lawn. He murmured, "David, I'm very glad that Nicholas told you about Frank."

And then, before Dave had time to even think about how to respond to that, Simon gestured towards the middle distance where a man was on his knees by a flower bed – and Nicholas was sitting cross–legged on the grass nearby wearing his Akubra but otherwise soaking up the sunshine. He looked so utterly relaxed.

"Thank you, Simon," said Dave. And Simon nodded his acknowledgement and headed back inside.

Dave took a moment to breathe in the fresh air and turn his face, as Nicholas was, to the sun. It was so much gentler here than in Australia. He liked it well enough, but figured it would take some getting used to. He set off across the lawn, watching his … whatever it was he and Nicholas were to each other. He doubted there were any words. Or none that wouldn't make him wince. Or blush.

Australians weren't meant to blush. They were going to put something in the Preamble to the Constitution about it.

Meanwhile, it seemed clear that Nicholas was basking in not just the sunshine but in Frank's presence, and in his own happiness, too. Dave liked to think that he himself might at least have something to do with the latter.

Nicholas finally saw him when Dave was about halfway across the lawn. He grinned impossibly bright, and scrambled up to his feet, jogged lightly over to meet him. There was confusion for a few moments of the most delightful kind. They were reaching for each other's hands and fumbling, not hugging but still drawing near and nearer; Dave was grinning like an idiot himself, they were both grinning too much to kiss, so they settled for resting temple against temple under the brim of Nicholas's Akubra and then twisting around, trying to see each other more clearly while staying in contact … It was ridiculous, really, and at last Nicholas just let out a joyous laugh, wrapped both of his arms tight around Dave's shoulders and gathered him in, and Dave wound his own arms around Nicholas's waist, and they just kind of clung and swayed together there as if they were utterly mad.

Which Dave supposed they were, really. In the best possible ways. This was love. If Dave had still had any qualms or questions, there could be no doubting the answers now.

Eventually Nicholas laughed again, and they broke apart – except that Nicholas kept one of Dave's hands in his, and tugged at it. "Come and meet Frank," he said, with a complete lack of guile.

"Sure," Dave replied easily. He didn't know if he was supposed to realise who Frank was, but that was fine. There was no need for any drama or fuss.

Frank was apparently weeding, grasping each invader in one gloved hand, and levering it out with a gardening fork in the other. He stopped what he was doing as Nicholas and Dave drew near, and stood, taking his gloves off. When Nicholas introduced them to each other, Frank shook Dave's hand with both of his own – and he called Dave 'sir' with a friendly smile. It seemed to be as Simon said, that everyone was happy to welcome him as Nicholas's … whatever. Future partner. There was no hint from Frank that there was anything particular about his relationship with Nicholas, but while the three of them exchanged inanities about the garden and the weather, Nicholas seemed both proud and bashful. And finally, when Dave happened to be turning to look back towards the house, he caught a glimpse from the corner of his eye of Frank winking broadly at Nicholas, as if to say 'Well done!' – and Nicholas gurgled a happy laugh in reply. Dave manfully pretended not to notice.

"*Anyway,*" said Nicholas rather heavily, as if needing to change the subject, "poor David has had to leave his beloved Land Cruiser behind in Australia –"

"Are you joking? I'm having it shipped out."

"So, *Frank*, I thought maybe you'd give him a tour of the cars sometime, and see if there's something that might distract him from the grief."

"Of course, Nicholas," Frank replied. "Tomorrow morning, perhaps, sir?"

"Um, after lunch would be better. If that doesn't get in the way of your work."

"Plans already?" Nicholas commented with a slightly quirked smile.

"Plans … jet lag …" Dave gestured vaguely: Who could possibly know?

They agreed that Nicholas would accompany Dave to the garage at around two–thirty the following afternoon. And then Frank added that if there were any motors that Dave took a shine to, there'd be no problem with him using them, working on them, driving them …

"Thanks," said Dave, quite genuinely. Though as he and Nicholas finally took their leave of Frank and started heading back towards the house, Dave complained, "I can't believe you want me to cheat on the Cruiser!"

"Aw, don't think of it like that … The Cruiser won't mind you having a meaningless holiday fling."

"Yeah, well, look how that worked out for you! And anyway," he continued, "if we're getting married or whatever, don't you want me to be the loyal type?"

"If … ?" Nicholas echoed, with a quiet little edge to it.

"Well, we are, aren't we?" Dave confirmed. "Getting married." He found himself literally scratching his head in puzzlement. "And I'm the loyal type. Whether that's Denise, or the Cruiser, or you … Wasn't that one of the first things you knew about me?"

Nicholas took Dave's hand, just very lightly, and stopped them both somewhere on the lawn between the flower beds and the terrace. "This got rather serious," he said with a solemn kind of humour. "I thought you'd enjoy seeing the cars, and maybe driving them. That's all."

"Yeah, that's fine," Dave replied, though he suspected there was more to it than that. "That's good."

"I really didn't mean it about you cheating on the Cruiser, you know."

Dave smiled. "That's even better."

Nicholas took a tiny step closer, suddenly seeming a little breathless. "I like you being loyal. I even liked that you were loyal to Denise – and still are!"

"I know." It was fine. He squeezed Nicholas's hand, and they turned to continue slowly on their way.

A long moment passed before Nicholas asked with deceptive lightness, "How long were you planning to stay?"

"Well …" He hardly knew how to answer that.

"I mean … you have a return ticket … ? Is it an open ticket, maybe?"

They hadn't talked about the future in anything but the most general terms. Dave cleared his throat, wondering if Nicholas could pick up on how nervous he was. Knowing that he probably could. "No, I don't."

"You don't – ?"

"Have a return ticket. But I *do* want to go back, right? I want – I'd really like it if we lived there. Nicholas, if you –"

"No, I want that, too. To live in Australia with you. In your home … ?"

"Yes. Please. Unless you –"

"No, I loved it there. I really did. Your family home."

"Good." Not that Dave had family any more, but it was the house in which he'd grown up. The house his parents had bought when they married. The house which, between the three of them over the years, they'd fixed up and made into something pretty special – though nothing to compare to an English manor house, of course.

"And – Well, if –" Now Nicholas cleared his throat. "Um – I don't understand. They let you into the country without a return airline ticket?"

"No. I, um – Well, I applied for a British passport before I left. I mean, I'm still Australian, but Dad was English, yeah? So I can be both, and I thought –"

"Oh, David!" Nicholas had stopped again, and was standing there staring at him with his eyes glowing. "That's marvellous!"

"It's one of the reasons I didn't come over right away. To be honest, it took me a while to realise I should, and then it took a few weeks to get the passport, but that was okay because I had to get things sorted out with the house. I did one trip I had booked, but there's another I'm meant to be doing in September."

"So we have until September?" It wasn't quite August yet.

"No, I've got – Well, there's a couple who help me out with the larger tour groups. They're gonna do this one for me."

Nicholas asked, kind of hushed, "How long were you planning to stay?"

"As long as it takes, I guess."

"Oh *God* …" Nicholas looked almost more overcome than he'd been when they'd been announcing – in front of Nicholas's entire family – their intention to marry. "Thank you. Oh David, *thank you*."

Dave cast a look about him as if there'd be some answer to the nervousness he felt. He hadn't counted on this meaning so much to Nicholas. Except he'd known that it would, hadn't he? "I figured the passport – I mean, having British citizenship or whatever – would make things more straightforward."

"It will. Oh, I'm sure it will. And you'll stay while we're planning the ceremony and everything?"

He sighed, and ventured, "We're not talking about just swinging by the registry office next time we're in town, are we?"

Nicholas shook his head very solemnly. No. No, they were not.

"How long are we talking about?"

"Six months?"

"All right," he said stoically. Six months of – he assumed – living in a mansion house with an Earl, with nothing to do all day but plan a big gay wedding and be tempted to cheat on the Cruiser. Well, he didn't suppose that was so bad.

"Can you do that? Do you have other trips planned for later in the year?"

"No, most people want to head up north – to places more like Kakadu, you know? But once the Wet starts, there's no point."

After a moment, Nicholas said a bit brokenly, "Can we go sit down? Inside?"

"Of course. Are you okay?" Dave asked in concern, following Nicholas towards the nearest door while managing to usher him in at the same time.

"Yes. Yes, I'm fine. I just – need a cold drink. I don't like to get too hot."

"You never said … How on earth did you cope in Australia, then?"

"I don't know. I don't know. That was different. And it was winter there!" Nicholas led the way into the family living room, and headed for the discreet little bar area while swiping off the Akubra.

Dave watched carefully as Nicholas put together two tall tumblers of ice, bottled water and lime juice. He needed to learn this kind of thing, for both their sakes. Though he reflected that he'd never had to push Nicholas to drink enough water in Australia, as he'd often had to with other clients from cooler countries. Now he guessed something of why.

Nicholas brought the drinks over, and collapsed to sprawl on a sofa, glancing at the seat beside him to indicate Dave should join him. A moment passed during which Nicholas cooled down, and even Dave sipped appreciatively at his drink. Eventually he asked again, "All right?"

"Yes." Nicholas nodded gently, not lifting his head from the back of the sofa. "It was different in Australia. It was an adventure – and I was so happy! And it'll be fine when we go back there."

"Brisbane, though," Dave said with fresh misgivings. "It was still pretty warm, wasn't it? Compared to the kind of winters you're used to. And you don't know what it's like in the summer. It can be pretty tough, even for those of us who are used to it. It's not just the heat, it's the humidity."

"Don't let's worry about that for now."

"What, then? What was the matter?"

"I just –" Nicholas gazed at him, more utterly vulnerable than beseeching, though it had the same effect. "Three months, if you want. Not six. But – you know what I'm talking about. Once I've gone, I might not get to come back. And I've *loved* it here, David. I *love* my family, I've *chosen* to stay here, it's not because I had to –"

"Oh God," he muttered, distraught.

"It's all right, though," said Nicholas. "It's all right, because I love being with you even more."

Dave just reached to hold his hand.

"So we'll do this, all right? But let me have this time. Share this time with me, be part of it with me. Let me make a bit of a fuss. I'll say goodbye properly. And then we can start our new life together, and it will be fine."

"Will it?" he asked.

"Yes," Nicholas replied with great certainty. "It will be *perfect*."

Dave groaned a little, completely out of words. And then he put the drink down, and crawled along the sofa to lie by his love with his head on Nicholas's chest listening to that strong patient heartbeat. Praying that it would never ever stop.

Late that night they made love in Nicholas's bed with the lights out, but with the curtains and windows open letting in the moonlight and the fresh night air. Soon – as he had a few times already in the past thirty-six hours – Nicholas was kneeling between Dave's thighs, rolling a condom onto himself. "We're getting married …" Nicholas mused. "We'll get the tests done. We won't have to use these any more." After a moment he added, "I've never fucked without one."

"You'll like it," said Dave.

"Will I?"

"I'm guessing … it'll be intense."

"Guessing?"

Dave shrugged. "Me and Denise – there was never anyone else. Didn't need them. I liked the – skin against skin. No barriers. Me and you –"

Nicholas belatedly understood. "You haven't had the chance to find out."

He sat back on his heels, considering Dave with a bit of a sour twist to his mouth. "You want to fuck me, David?"

"Wouldn't be many men who'd say no to that. But not if you don't want to."

"I've never – I've never actually done that." Nicholas drifted further into thought, his brow wrinkling in a frown, though his cock still stood proud and rubber–wrapped between them. "Don't know why, really …"

Dave wondered if he was misremembering. "You offered once before, didn't you? In Charleville, the night you first fucked me."

"Did I … ? Well, I suppose … it felt like a night on which *something* significant should happen." Nicholas appeared rather troubled by the recollection.

"Hey, if it's not your thing, it's not a problem," Dave assured him, shifting up onto his elbows and reaching for the man. "Come on, don't leave me hanging here."

Nicholas's attention returned, and he slowly eased forward into place, shifting over Dave as if he were prowling, his focus becoming curious, engaged. "You like this, yes?"

He shivered, already losing himself. "Yes. Already lost count – since I got here –"

A gut–deep groan wrenched itself out of Nicholas. "I'm – Oh God! Maybe I shouldn't –"

"You bloody well should," Dave insisted in a vehement whisper.

"Shouldn't overdo it," Nicholas was muttering, even as they both moved into place. They already knew this so very well. "Don't want to hurt you."

"Don't care if you make me feel it, Nicholas. Never thought about it before –"

"Before … ?"

"Before there was you." His thighs gripping either side of Nicholas's waist, his stomach muscles curling him up, lifting his hips, ready to receive the man. "Before you made me such a slut for it."

Nicholas groaned again, and surged forward. "You're sure?" he asked, hesitating at the last possible moment.

"Do it," said Dave. And they both cried out as Nicholas impaled him.

two

Dave woke at a far more reasonable hour the next morning, and shared a late breakfast with Nicholas, before making his excuses and heading off to meet Simon at eleven. He figured he'd tell Nicholas about it afterwards.

Simon was waiting for him in the main hall, and showed Dave through to the neat little office just beyond the hidden door. "How may I help you, David?" he asked in a warm yet professional manner once they'd both sat down.

"It's about Nicholas," Dave blurted out.

Simon didn't even blink. "Yes, of course."

"It's about – He told me about – about the brain aneurysm, you see. And I wanted to make sure that I understood. I figured – you'd have made it your job to know what to do, what to be careful of. I want to make sure I know that, too."

About halfway through this stumbling explanation, Simon had begun smiling softly, and after a brief pause he said, "Nicholas has made a very good choice in you, hasn't he?"

Dave coloured up, and remained silent, though to himself he fervently swore, *'God, I hope so.'*

"If I know anything about you, Mr Taylor," Simon continued, "I would guess you've already done your homework."

"Yes. I know that only one in twelve– or thirteen–thousand people have a ruptured aneurysm each year in England."

"And in Nicholas's case, it's a small aneurysm, sir. A diameter of less than seven millimetres."

"Oh. Good." He hadn't known that. Cerebral aneurysms could measure even five centimetres or more, and of course the larger they got the more dangerous they were.

"He has it monitored, and he's on medication. I'm sure you'll support him in that, though Nicholas takes the matter quite as seriously as you'd wish him to."

"But he hasn't had surgery to fix it."

"The balance of risks doesn't make surgery worthwhile – under present circumstances. It might become more desirable later. But I'm afraid that even surgery wouldn't entirely fix the problem, David; it would only reduce the likelihood of rupture."

Dave nodded. Things weren't quite as bleak as he'd feared, though it was bad enough. "The problem is …" he slowly continued, "if something happens, if it ruptures, there probably won't be anything I can do about it. And I hate that."

"Of course there'll be plenty to do, sir," Simon briskly replied. "You'll need to immediately call for an ambulance. The emergency number is 999 here in England."

"Yes."

"He will be – I'm sorry, sir, but you'd best be prepared. Nicholas will probably be in a great deal of pain. They describe it as … beyond the most excruciating of headaches. You'll need to take care of him. He'll be disoriented. He might lapse into unconsciousness. And he might vomit, so you'll need to make sure his airways remain clear. But I know you have a current first aid certificate, so you'll know what to do."

"Of course. Yes." Dave swallowed, not liking at all to think of Nicholas in agonising pain, and probably terrified as well. But Simon was right – it was better to imagine it now, and not be shocked or panicked into being good for nothing at the time. "The – the recovery position. Will be useful."

"Just so. He'll be in good hands with you, David, until the medical personnel arrive. I have no fears for him on that account. And I'm sure he'll find your presence a great comfort."

He asked, "Is there anything else I should know?"

"I don't think so, sir. It seems you're aware of the important matters, and I'm sure your research has detailed far more."

Dave was quiet for a time. Mentally girding himself. Hoping that such preparation would never be called on. At last he thought to say, "If his family are concerned – Would you reassure them? I'll do my very best for him. I really will."

"They know as much, sir, but I'll tell Lord Goring that we've spoken, if I may."

"Of course."

Another pause lengthened. Dave must have been looking a bit lost, as Simon softly said, "Don't worry unnecessarily, Dave. Nicholas leads a healthy life. He does what he can to minimise the potential for problems.

And he's still young. There'll be time to worry more when he's older."

"I hope so. Yes."

"There's every chance that he'll enjoy a long life. Whatever happens, though, if he's shared his life with you, then he'll want for nothing more. He'll have no regrets."

Dave had coloured up again, but he glanced at Simon and nodded his thanks.

"And you, sir?" Simon asked lightly. "Are you all right? It can't be easy for you. Nicholas isn't the only person for us to worry about."

Which Dave appreciated, he really did, though he brushed off Simon's concern. "Oh, *I'll* be all right. Like you said: nothing more. I don't want for anything more."

"Then bless you, Dave, for being your own good self."

At which point Dave stood, muttered his thanks, shook Simon's hand, and made himself scarce.

There didn't seem to be any order in which the extended family sat down for meals, with three exceptions: Richard, the earl, always sat at the head of the table; Robert, his eldest son and heir, always sat somewhere around the middle; and Robert's wife Penelope always sat at the far end. Dave assumed that Penelope had become the lady of the house after Nicholas's mother died a few years before.

Otherwise, people sat quite randomly, depending on whim or on who they were already having a conversation with. It had felt a bit disorienting at first, but Dave soon decided he liked the informality – especially when contrasted with the dauntingly old dining room, where they were surrounded by the sort of tapestries and paintings Dave associated with the dustiest museums. There was a great long table set with fine china that put the set he'd inherited from his grandmother to shame, and glasses that were probably crystal or something – different sizes and shapes for different drinks – and cutlery that was probably real silver. Still, everyone seemed far more concerned about having fun – and talking over each other and making sure the kids were okay – than bothering over whether Dave was using the right knife.

As they gathered for lunch that day, Richard came into the room just after Dave and Nicholas, and murmured, "Perhaps you'd sit by me today, David."

"Oh. Sure. Thanks." He looked at Nicholas's father, and saw at a glance that Simon must have already told Richard of his conversation with Dave. Richard looked back at him with solemn gratitude, and nodded. Then a sweeping gesture invited him to sit at the earl's right – which even Dave knew was a place of privilege. He'd been invited to sit there for the first family dinner he'd attended, as well.

Nicholas didn't seem to make anything of it, other than perhaps accepting this as Dave's due. He followed Dave, though chatting away to his sister Lilibet, and claimed the seat to Dave's right by standing there with his hands on the back of the chair. Young Robin made the most of Nicholas's distraction, however, by nipping in to sit down beside Dave.

"Oh! Cheeky!" cried Nicholas – who promptly made sure to claim the next chair along. Lilibet sat on his far side, and picked up the briefly interrupted conversation.

Robin chuckled in glee, and grinned winningly at Dave. Robin was all of ten years old, and the most delightfully innocent flirt. Dave smiled back at him, and winked, which made the boy chuckle again.

"Robin," said Richard, "perhaps you'd let Nicholas and David enjoy being together for this little while. I suppose it mightn't mean very much to some, but they recently became engaged."

Nicholas glanced at Dave, though he must already know that Dave didn't mind. It wasn't as if Dave didn't have plenty of Nicholas's undivided attention at other times … "It's all right, Father. I can share. *To a point*," Nicholas added in ironically severe tones to Robin.

"You'd think Robin would be jealous," one of the other adults commented. A sister–in–law, Dave thought. Which would make her Amanda or Christine.

"You'd think he'd hate him," someone else down the far end of the table muttered under his breath.

Robert commented, "Oh, I think Robin saw pretty quickly that he'd lost that one – and if you can't beat 'em, join 'em!"

And Robin was still beaming at Dave almost as broadly as Nicholas did, apparently perfectly used to being teased about his partialities. Dave laughed, and chucked him under the chin – and wondered if Robin mightn't faint with happiness.

Once they'd all been served and were more settled, Richard asked Dave and Nicholas, "Have you two made any plans?"

"Uh – Tour of the garage this afternoon," Dave supplied. Too late, he realised what Richard really meant, and feebly concluded, "I hear you have quite a collection of cars."

"We do. Rather an indulgence in this day and age, I'm afraid, but please make yourself at home there, if that's where your interests lie."

"Thank you. I will."

After a moment Nicholas answered the real question. "I know it's not much time to organise everything, Father, but we thought we'd hold the wedding in three months, if that's all right –"

"Six months," Dave quietly put in. "We talked about *six* months."

"No, it's fine," Nicholas reassured him. "Three months. Apart from anything else, I'd like to have the reception in the garden, and late October is probably doable, but winter certainly isn't!" Upon which thought he got distracted by his own fancies. "Although what if it snowed … ? That would be amazing! A real white wedding! Like in *Camelot*, you know? With the sled and the furs …"

"A *white* wedding," someone muttered, and someone else snorted – and Dave felt like hitting them, family or not. He remembered Denise once remarking, '*Everyone* deserves to wear white on their wedding day, if that's what they want.'

Penelope said, rather more reasonably, "Nicholas, I don't think even you could stage manage the weather, I'm sorry, and a slushy wedding would be so *dreary*."

Nicholas laughed under his breath, though it sounded a bit forced. "All right, the end of October. Reception in the garden, if we can."

"And the ceremony?" Richard asked.

"Just a few of us in town, I thought – the two of us and witnesses – and then come back to everyone here." He turned on his seat towards Dave. "We haven't talked about this yet. You'd better tell us what you'd like."

"It's fine," Dave said. "Sounds good so far." Though he took the opportunity to lean in closer over Robin's head and mutter, "Don't have to wear white, do I? Or *do* I … ?"

Nicholas laughed more genuinely, and answered so that everyone might hear him. "No, we'll wear morning suits. You'll look very dapper, I promise."

"*Mourning* suits … ?"

"No, uh – I –" Nicholas gestured at himself, as if about to launch into an explanation, before realising it was hopeless. "We can talk about that later. I'll show you mine – though of course I'd like for us all to have new ones."

"Right," said Dave, a bit shortly. Hadn't he already told Nicholas that he'd never once worn a suit? If he hadn't worn one for his dad's funeral, then he didn't see why he should wear one now.

The pause threatened to become a difficult silence, until Richard smoothly asked, "Wouldn't you like to hold the ceremony here as well, Nicholas? That would seem appropriate."

"Ah, but we'd have to apply for a licence to hold weddings and partnership ceremonies, and that would mean *anyone* could get hitched here, so – unless you want to go into business as an event venue … ?"

"Ah. Maybe not. What a pity! It would have been nice to have it all here."

"It'll be nice in town, too. Do you remember they have rooms set up at the old courthouse?"

"Yes, of course."

"There's the Disraeli Room on weekdays," Nicholas chattered on, "and Midsomer Court on Fridays and weekends. Midsomer Court has the nicer name, but it looks kind of plain judging from the photos. Though there's this terrific light coming in through the high windows … The Disraeli Room is older, and more what I imagined. Like I said, though, it depends on the exact day we're doing this …" He finally trailed off, seeing that everyone was watching him in amusement. "What?"

"You've researched this, then," Robert commented.

"Yeah."

"Wondered what you were both doing up there in your room for all those hours …" This was greeted with guffaws from various adults around the table.

Nicholas sniffed and said primly, "David was sleeping off his jet lag, so I had to occupy myself *somehow* …"

"All right, all right," said Richard, quite amicably. "That's enough of that. Simon, perhaps it's time to clear the plates?"

"Oh!" Nicholas exclaimed as they were walking through the house after lunch. "I can show you …" He took Dave's hand and led him round a corner and into what seemed to be a study or maybe even a small library. A profusion of framed photos covered a great deal of one wall. Nicholas only took a moment to find the one he was looking for. "See? This was Robert and Penelope's wedding. We're all in morning suits. It's what's expected, it's traditional, but really I just love it. Everyone looks so smart!"

"Well," Dave admitted, "you *do* look smart." All the men in the photo looked very – whatever that word Nicholas used was. Dapper. They were very dapper – and especially Nicholas with his tall slim frame and his broad shoulders. But even Robert looked great, despite the fact he tended to appear as if he'd just been hauled backwards out of a rugby scrum – and the rather sturdy Richard was every inch the Earl.

"I jump at any excuse to wear Morning Grey, to be honest – I prefer that to the traditional black jacket and striped trousers like Robert and my father are in here, and I figure it's our wedding so we can just go with the grey if we want to – but we can add a bit of colour to things with the ties and waistcoats, if you like. Hey! Maybe, like, a rainbow of colours – subtle colours, I mean, but each of us in a different colour of the rainbow." Nicholas nudged him with an elbow. "Gay pride, you know?"

"Yeah. I get it."

After a pause that became a bit too lengthy, Nicholas said, "Well, we don't have to wave the whole Gay Pride flag thing, but *God* you'll look gorgeous in a morning suit, David. I promise you will."

"They have *tails*," he complained.

"A cutaway skirt," said Nicholas.

"A skirt! Like *that* makes it better." Dave sighed, and took a step back. Considered Nicholas, and tried to judge just how important this was to him compared to how important it was to himself. They seemed equally determined at this point. "I think I told you already," Dave eventually said, "I've never worn a suit before."

"There's a first time for everything," Nicholas remarked – and he made his point by complacently patting Dave's rear. "As well you know."

"Nicholas. I just don't do suits."

"But –"

"You look great," Dave said, indicating the photo again. "You really do.

But my idea of dressing up is the white shirt and jeans I wore on the first day I came here."

Nicholas's mouth pinched up unhappily. "You're not suggesting," he slowly responded, "that you wear *jeans* for our wedding … ?"

"Well, no," said Dave, privately thinking that actually he'd be perfectly happy with the kind of wedding where *everyone* wore jeans. "I don't know, all right? Not jeans. But … not a suit either."

Nicholas let out a gusted sigh. "All right. Well. We'll have to think about that, then."

"*You* can still wear a morning suit, can't you? If that's what makes you happy?"

That earned him a smile, tiny but genuine, and Nicholas reached to hold Dave's hand again. "All right. Come on," he continued rather more robustly. "Let's not keep Frank waiting."

Dave was given a tour of the old stable block which had been converted to, among other things, a working garage and a display area for an impressive range of cars. Frank led the way, while Dave followed with Nicholas tagging along after him. Dave and Nicholas held hands the entire time. Perhaps they needed the mutual reassurance. Frank seemed like a fairly quiet man by nature, but it didn't take much to get him talking. He provided a potted history for each car, and lovingly listed both their strengths and their weaknesses. He had polishing cloths stowed in a pocket, and at the slightest provocation would haul them out, one in each hand, and buff the paintwork and chrome.

When they reached the Rolls Royce Silver Cloud, Dave was way more impressed than he thought he'd be. "That's something," was his verdict.

"Yes, sir, it is."

Dave turned to Nicholas. "You said we'll be going into town for the ceremony … ?"

"Yes. We'll be going to Beaconsfield."

"Will we go in this … ?"

Nicholas was suddenly beaming again. "*God*, yes!"

"There you go. Got that sorted."

And with a pealing laugh, Nicholas slid his arms around Dave's waist, and clung on, tucking his head in beside Dave's like they'd never be parted again.

"And for the honeymoon, sir?" Frank smoothly asked after a moment or two. "Will the two of you be driving somewhere?"

"I don't know! Nicholas? I haven't had much of a chance to think about any of this."

"Because I thought, sir, that you might like to take the Jaguar XJ."

"Oh!" Dave looked back down the line of gleaming bonnets to where the Jaguar waited, ready to prowl. "In that case, yes, I think we *will* be driving somewhere, absolutely!"

"I'll have you added to the family's insurance policy, sir. Shouldn't take more than a phone call."

"Thank you. Really, thanks. That's great."

Nicholas clung on even harder, and Dave found himself pressing a kiss to the man's dark hair, just instinctively and without embarrassment.

"So, then you have *that* sorted out as well, sir," said Frank with a certain sense of satisfaction.

It seemed, for now at least, that the wedding was the main topic of conversation for the entire family – though Nicholas was no doubt the only one of them to find it so endlessly fascinating. Over dinner that evening, Richard said, "David, forgive me for not asking before. I assume you'll be inviting guests from Australia?"

"Oh. Yes." They'd already established that Dave had no 'real' family any more, being the only child of parents who'd died – his mother when he was just a boy. But that didn't mean he didn't have *family*. "My friend Denise," he said, "and her husband and daughter. Well, Zoe is still a baby, but she can travel, can't she?" He looked about him, figuring that someone in the Goring family would know the answer to that. "She'll be … getting on for six months old in October."

Penelope said, "I'm sure that'll be fine, David."

There were other assenting murmurs around the table. Someone chipped in, "Prudence came to Germany with us when she wasn't even *three* months." – "Oh, that explains it," someone else teased.

"Zoe is a healthy baby … ?" Penelope asked, smoothly ignoring the repartee.

"Yes. Well, as far as I know," he added, though he figured that Denise would have told him if there was anything very wrong. Zoe was his godchild, after all – on an informal basis anyway. "She seemed to be thriving last Saturday!" God, he thought … was it really less than a week ago that he'd been in Australia?

"I'm sure she'll be fine. It will be lovely to meet your friends."

"And there's Charlie, as well," Dave continued. "I'd like to invite Charlie. I don't know that he'd want to bring anyone. And that's probably about it."

"Excellent," said Richard. "They'd be very welcome to stay here with us, if that's what they'd like. There's plenty of room, certainly for another four."

"Oh. Thank you. That's very good of you."

"Perhaps you'll let them know. You must phone them whenever you like. Nicholas, we really ought to be sending out invitations, as soon as you've decided on a date."

"I'm on it, Father!"

There was some wry chuckling and comments such as "Of course he is" from around the table.

Nicholas ignored them, and was instead contemplating Dave. After a moment, he asked, "Who'll be your witness?"

"Denise." This was met with a nod, as if Nicholas had known the answer all along. Dave asked, "Who'll be yours?"

"Robert." Nicholas looked across the table at his eldest brother. "If you will … ?"

"I'd be honoured," said Robert in low fervent tones. The two of them each stood, and shook hands across the table. Such an honestly felt moment moved everyone, and there was a respectful silence for a while as the brothers sat back down again.

Dave sighed, and reflected that if it was evening here in England then it must be early morning in Australia. He'd see Simon about phoning Denise once dinner was over, though he'd have to figure out how to cover the costs of the call. Denise hadn't heard his news yet, though he knew she wouldn't be surprised. And in any case … he missed her.

"You little beauty!" was Denise's reaction to his announcement. "I knew it!"

"I know you knew it. And you were right."

"Still. That was fast work."

Dave could hear his own chuckle echoing down the line. "Mate, I was engaged within about five minutes of walking into the house."

She made some more jubilant noises, and hollered out the news to Vittorio, before at last saying rather more seriously, "Davey, I'm really happy for you, mate."

"Thanks, Denny." He smiled, imagining her smiling. Not that he had to imagine it, really, as he could hear it in her voice.

"And you're happy, right?" Denise continued.

"Yeah. Yeah, I am."

"So, have you, like, started talking about dates and things … ? I suppose it's a bit soon to be getting into all that!"

Dave snorted. "*Yeah*, we've been talking dates … The ceremony's at eleven a.m. on the thirty–first of October, in the Disraeli Room at the old magistrate's courthouse in Beaconsfield. Which is somewhere near here, in Buckinghamshire. We haven't formally registered our notice, or whatever it is, but Nicholas called to make sure the time was available, and we're going in to fix it up as soon as we can. Apparently we can't do that until I've been here for nine days, or whatever."

There was a brief pause, before Denise said, "Oh."

"After the ceremony, the reception's in the garden back here at the house." Then he burst out, "God, *tell* me you'll be here, Denise. Tell me you'll come. With Zoe and Vittorio, too, of course. I'm gonna ask Charlie as well. You can all stay here at the house – Richard said you should. The Earl, I mean. My future father–in–law! Denise –"

"Of *course* we'll be there, Davey. Of *course* we will."

"And you'll be my witness, like you said."

"Oh, Davey mate," she said quietly, almost sorrowfully, "of course I will. I'll *always* stand beside you. That's what I said, and I meant it."

"Good," he said. "Good."

Another pause lengthened. Eventually Denise asked, "Are you all right, Davey? I mean, I know you're happy about Nicholas, but … are you all right otherwise?"

"I guess."

"Now, come on, don't clam up like a big dumb Aussie male on me now.

You're made of sterner stuff, mate."

In almost no time at all, Dave was confessing, "I just don't like being the centre of attention, you know? I mean, if I'd been marrying you, *you'd* be the centre of attention, cos you'd be the bride! But here —"

"Are you telling me you feel like you're the bride in this, Davey?"

"*No. God*, no. I'm not. And I'm not talking about what goes on in bed or anything —"

"Uh huh."

"Just … God, they're *all* here. The entire family. Not to mention the servants, for God's sake. Servants! And everyone's curious, and when they're around Nicholas hardly talks about anything other than the wedding, and —"

"Are they treating you okay? Is anyone giving you grief?"

"No grief at all. They're all really happy about it. They're *staggeringly* open-minded about the whole gay thing."

"Well, look. Don't you think it will be, like, a seven-day wonder? If they're that cool, then it won't take long before you just fit in, and you're part of the family already. Then it won't be such an issue, right?"

"Right," he agreed, though doubtingly.

"Just give it a few more days, love. Once the planning's properly underway for the wedding, and once people are used to having you around, I bet it'll be fine. And in the meantime, maybe you and Nicholas could go do some sightseeing, or something? Find an excuse to get out of the house for a while, you know? With just the two of you."

Dave grinned down the phone. "Denny, you're brilliant. Of course that's what we'll do. That's just *brilliant*."

"Any time, mate."

"So, look," he said. "Seeing as you're such a genius, you have to help me find something to wear for the wedding that isn't jeans and isn't a morning suit."

"A *mourning* suit?"

"I know, right? That's what I said!" And he explained the situation, and how he didn't want to let Nicholas down, but he just couldn't wear a suit, and eventually Denise said very seriously, "Let me think about it, all right? We'll come up with something, I promise. But give me a few days to think about it."

"God, thank you *so much*," he said. "Love you, Denny."

"Love you, too, mate. Always."

And finally they said their goodbyes and hung up.

three

The next day, with Nicholas happily curled up beside him in the passenger seat, Dave carefully drove the Jaguar XJ out of the garage and down the gravel driveway. Frank stood there watching them go – Dave glimpsed him in the wing mirror – Frank's smile happy yet with a slight poignancy to it which Dave wondered was more about Nicholas or more about the car.

"Okay. Where are we going?" Dave asked as they reached the road that ran past the mansion house.

"You wanted sky –"

"Well, just a bit more of it. You know what Aussie skies are like." England's skies were mild and pleasant but seemed so much smaller. Which was probably impossible, but also undeniably true.

"It's all right. I can give you sky. Turn left," said Nicholas. Once Dave had done so, Nicholas announced, "We're going to Ivinghoe Beacon."

Which didn't mean anything at all to Dave, but between the satnav and Nicholas's supplementary guidance, he got them there safely – and the Jaguar proved to be a sinfully smooth way of doing so. Ivinghoe Beacon turned out to be the last hill of a long curving range. Once they'd climbed the chalky paths to the top, then all of Buckinghamshire and probably a fair bit beyond it lay spread before them like a patchwork quilt in greens and browns. Importantly, there was plenty of sky, and with their backs turned to the other hills, it felt as if the earth had risen beneath their feet and thrust them halfway up into the air.

The two of them ended up sitting on the grassy slope just beyond the edge of the hilltop, just before it got steep. Nicholas lay back to dream up into the sky, while Dave simply gazed at the horizon, so very much more distant than the other English horizons he'd encountered so far.

After a while, Nicholas's hand slipped into Dave's, and they continued there connected in a companionable silence, not caring if they startled the nearby model plane enthusiasts who were making great use of updrafts on the north side of the hill. Occasionally a plane swooped past them or circled above. Not exactly butterflies, but they'd do!

Eventually Nicholas asked, "What d'you think?"

"It's great. Thanks. Just what I needed."

A brief pause before Nicholas continued, "This is one end of an old path called the Ridgeway. It leads down across England all the way to Avebury in Wiltshire. There's a stone circle there that you've probably heard of, or seen pictures of. Though I think the path originally continued on right down to the coast in Devon or Dorset or somewhere. It's been used for thousands of years."

"Cool," said Dave.

"I know it's not anything like your Australian songlines – it's more of a practical road, really – but I thought you'd like it."

"I do." He clasped Nicholas's hand tighter for a moment, as the man seemed to need reassurance. "And you know, songlines were practical, too."

Nicholas abruptly sat up. "God, you've only been here a few days, and you're already finding it a bit much, aren't you? I mean, my family and everything."

"Well," he started slowly … "I guess I am used to living on my own. And in my own house. But that's okay."

"It's not usually like this. Even when we try to all get together, it's rare that everyone's there. But it won't be for much longer. Lilibet and her lot are heading home tomorrow, and Michael is, too, because of work, though Amanda and the kids are staying on for an extra couple of days. It won't be long before it's just, well, the six of us – seven, with you – and Simon and so on. I suppose even that's going to be too much for you at times!"

"It'll be fine," Dave insisted. "Just maybe if we can do this sort of thing every now and then. If it can be just us two sometimes."

"Of course. Of course. We can go chasing butterflies, while the weather's still warm."

"Sure. I'll drive you wherever you like. See a bit of the country."

"What else d'you want to do?"

"You," said Dave in his best deadpan. "I want to do you."

Nicholas snorted. "And in between times … ?"

"Whatever you're doing. Planning the wedding and all that. Potting orchids. Teasing Robin. Housework! I'm used to looking after my own place, remember. Do the servants do *everything* for you?"

"Not everything, no."

"So I'll help with that – or the cars, or the garden. And otherwise we can just hang out."

"For three months?"

Dave shrugged. "Well, we just hung out at the waterhole, didn't we? That wasn't so bad."

"It wasn't, was it?" Nicholas sighed. "And what you said before? You must know … I want it to be just the two of us."

"I know you love your family, Nicholas. I know you need to be with them, too. It's obvious you all get on really well." He sighed. "I really get that, you know. I don't remember much about my mum, but I know we were happy. And I adored my dad. He was my best friend." Dave confessed, "I don't know that I'd have been willing to leave him behind. Even for you."

"Oh, *David.*" Nicholas leaned in closer, and wrapped a firm arm around Dave's shoulders. "It'll break my heart to leave my father, like I know it would have broken yours. But there's one major difference."

"What's that?"

"Your father only had you. It was just the two of you, and Denise. Of course you couldn't have left him. My father has three other sons and a daughter, and all but one are married or as good as, and they've all got children. He'll hardly even notice I'm gone."

"You know he will," Dave said roughly, "cos you're the one he loves best."

Nicholas echoed in a forlorn little voice, "I'm the one he loves best."

"But he's a really decent guy, isn't he? He wants you to be happy. More than anything."

"And I'm happy with you, David. I'm happiest with you."

"I know." And they sat together there, hand in hand, halfway up in the sky.

Dave wasn't sure what woke him up that night. Nicholas was at his computer with the desk lamp on, but that wasn't anything very unusual. What with the last lingering effects of Dave's jet lag, and their spontaneous bouts of sex and napping, neither of them were keeping regular hours. But Nicholas wasn't just reading or surfing or answering emails – he was upset about something. Dave could tell from his edgy posture, if nothing else.

"Hey, what's up?" Dave murmured, shifting onto his elbows and trying to focus properly. "Nicholas?"

"Nothing. It's fine." Nicholas turned his head to offer a smile which was patently false. "It's fine, David. Go back to sleep."

Bugger that for an idea. Dave hauled himself up out of the bed, and padded over to rest his hands on Nicholas's shoulders, to lean in and find out what had troubled his love. He wasn't very surprised to discover an Australian Government website on the screen, and specifically a page titled *Visas, Immigration and Refugees*. "Ah. That's something I haven't looked into yet, I have to say. Except I worked out that at least they treat us like any other de facto couple. They'll give us a fair go, Nicholas, even if they don't consider us married."

The man looked up at him woefully, with his hands knotted together in his lap. "They want us to have lived together for twelve months before I can apply for a visa as your partner, and I doubt they'll count the time we spent together in Australia. I'd been thinking we could go live there right after our honeymoon, but if – Well, I know you can't stay here with me for a whole year. You have a business to run! Not to mention a life."

"Nah, there has to be a way. Look –" Dave glanced around, but he already knew there wasn't another straight–back chair in the room. "Look, bring that over here and sit with me. We'll work this out."

Dave ended up tucked into an armchair, with Nicholas curled up beside him with his thighs across Dave's lap, and the computer balanced somehow between them. "Okay," said Dave. "So, you need a Partner visa, right?"

"Yes. I can apply for a temporary one either while we're here or while we're in Australia, and it lasts for two years, and then if we're still together –"

"Which we will be."

"– which we will be, they'll consider making it permanent."

"So far, so good."

"We have to prove that we have a real relationship."

Various untoward thoughts drifted through his head. "Um …"

Nicholas shook with a weak chuckle. "Mind out of the gutter, David Taylor. I'm talking statements from friends, and a joint bank account."

"We'll go open one tomorrow."

"But there's still this twelve–month rule. I can't ask you to stay here with me, and my current visa only lets me stay in Australia for up to three months at a time … I don't see how we're going to even make this work at all!"

"I realise there are going to be hoops we need to jump through, but they can't have made it completely impossible!"

"Can't they?" Nicholas asked darkly.

"Show me the page." And Dave watched as Nicholas clicked through a number of screens before he settled on *Eligibility*, and scrolled down. "So … there's a waiver of the twelve months if we have children, if your partner – that's me – holds a humanitarian visa – which obviously I don't – or … if we've registered our de facto relationship."

"But that's in Australia. The civil partnership doesn't count!"

"All right," Dave said soothingly. "No worries. Let's see if we can do this registration thing as well." He freed his arm from around Nicholas's waist, opened a new tab in the browser, and soon found the right pages on the Queensland Government site. He read through them – silently this time – and concluded, "This will work. Only one of us has to already live there, and there's nothing to say we couldn't apply right away. And that means we can see about waiving the twelve months."

Nicholas was still gazing at him rather woefully, as if convinced it was never going to happen.

Dave gathered his thoughts. "Tell me why this won't work, then: We go ahead with the civil partnership ceremony. That's got to count as proof of our commitment, if nothing else. After the honeymoon, we travel to Australia. You still have your short–term visa from when you came out in May, right? So you can travel on that. As soon as we're settled, we register our relationship. Then you apply for a Partner visa. And we get on with life."

Hope was dawning on Nicholas's mutable face, though he warned, "It costs almost four thousand dollars to apply."

Dave didn't even blink. "So? I've got the money – and I'd pay a damned sight more than that to keep you with me."

Nicholas began smiling helplessly.

"It'll work!" Dave insisted.

But then the dawning smile faltered. "No, it won't. I can't stay longer than three months on my tourist visa, and they take up to six months to process a Partner visa application!"

Dave's face fell, too, for a moment – but then he rallied. "Look, if they're going to take that long, that's not our problem, is it? Surely there's a way of applying to extend your visa, or getting some other kind of temporary visa – all completely legit – while we're waiting for the outcome."

The outcome.

The words hung between them for a long moment. Nicholas whispered, "What if they don't approve it?"

"They will."

"But what if they don't?"

"Well, I'm a British citizen, too, remember? I'll come live here with you. Maybe not *here* here," he added, casting a glance at the huge old mansion house surrounding them. "But, you know. *Here.*"

"You'd really give up Australia … ?"

"For you, Nicholas," Dave said, in deceptively light tones, "I'd even give up Australia."

They stared at each other solemnly. Nicholas's eyes grew damp, and Dave's started prickling a little.

"So," Dave continued rather more robustly, "the Department of Immigration doesn't scare me. It'll cost a bit, and take a bit of work, but we'll jump through the hoops. And in the meantime we can have fun gathering evidence to prove our relationship. Like …" He cast around him, but didn't have to look far. There was a tiny camera lens in the lid of the laptop. "Like photos. We can take a photo of us here together right now, and it'll be date-stamped and everything. And we already have a couple of others, don't we? Lilibet took photos of us on that first night with your dad, and you took one of us with your phone when we were on the Beacon today."

By this time Nicholas was grinning in delight. "We'll take a photo every day!" he said. "You know, one a day, but at different times and places." His long pale fingers were calling up the laptop's camera even as he spoke. "And I could start up a blog! Yes, that's what I'll do. I'll blog every day, about us, and about all of what we're going through. That'll be proof, won't it?"

"It sounds *perfect.*"

Nicholas tucked his head in beside Dave's, adjusted the angle of the computer, and they both grinned while the camera faked a shutter sound. There wasn't enough light in the room for a quality photo, but their happiness came shining through sure enough. "That really is perfect," said Nicholas, so quietly that he himself might not have been aware of it. He carefully saved the photo, and then closed the laptop's lid. "Let's go to bed," he said, in rather more normal tones.

"You," said Dave, "always with the good ideas …"

"Ah, but in this case, it definitely takes two."

It wasn't that night but on another one not long after, that Dave felt like rewarding Nicholas. Dave was supposed to be the organised one of the pair of them, but Nicholas had been as good as his word; he'd set up his blog on wordpress.com, chosen a theme he liked, and diligently made an entry every day, each featuring a photograph of the two of them. He'd even created extra entries to cover the preceding few days, though being absolutely scrupulous about not fudging the date and time stamps on either the photos or the posts – and he was planning to also start a sequence of posts telling his story about how they'd first met and got together. His writing style was charmingly chatty and easy to read, no matter whether he was talking about Dave or their wedding plans or the visa rigmarole, describing where they'd gone that day, or waxing lyrical about butterflies. Dave figured that only an immigration officer without a soul could possibly remain unmoved or unconvinced. Dave himself was so moved that he'd had to force himself not to comment on the posts, for fear of making a complete arse of himself. About which he just couldn't tell any more.

On a more pragmatic level, Nicholas had realised they couldn't open a joint bank account until Dave could provide proof of where he was living. So Nicholas had made an appointment to introduce him to the family solicitors in order to ask for a formal letter to confirm matters. In response to which, Dave had said, "I should see about making a new will. I guess we can get things started on that while we're there, as well, yeah?"

Nicholas had gaped at him and then frowned in thought for a long moment, before tentatively asking, "What were you intending to … ?"

"Well, right now, it would all go to Denise or Zoe. But you should be my main beneficiary, shouldn't you?"

Nicholas still seemed surprisingly unsure about something. "Because it will be evidence of us being in a committed relationship? For the Department of Immigration, I mean."

"No, because that's the way it should be," Dave corrected him. "We're getting married, aren't we?"

"Yes, we are." Nicholas finally broke into a big happy grin. "I'll do the same."

"But getting married doesn't change the fact that Zoe's kind of my godchild, right?"

"Of course not! It means she'll be kind of mine as well. If Denise and Vittorio don't mind."

"They won't mind," Dave said, very lightly. So once things were finalised and signed and witnessed, other than a substantial bequest to Zoe, Nicholas would receive all Dave's worldly possessions when he died.

Nicholas did likewise, though he chose to leave some personal gifts to Robin rather than money. "It's not like he won't have plenty anyway," Nicholas explained to Dave. "He's in line for the whole shebang one day. So you might as well have what's mine. And there's a fair bit, you know. I haven't had my own family to raise, like the others, and I've never had my own home to pay for."

"As long as you know that's not why I'm marrying you."

"No, it's for the sex, isn't it?"

"Yes, Nicholas. It's for the sex."

Well, whether it was or it wasn't, Dave wanted to offer something to Nicholas as a reward. Late one night as they drifted together down the river that was making love, Dave with Nicholas, this wondrous river already so familiar – just as the current started to tug them into deeper stronger waters, Dave murmured, "What d'you want to do? Nicholas? What do you want that we haven't done yet?"

"Oh God," Nicholas complained half–seriously against Dave's throat, "you're bored with me already."

"You *know* I'm not." He tried to explain while Nicholas resumed the lovely distraction of his mouthings and gnawings. "I just thought … if there was something different … you might want … as well as, I mean. Not instead of."

Nicholas finally pulled back a little to consider him, and they gently floated back into relative calm. A long serious moment later, Nicholas asked, "Anything?"

"Anything," he promised with perfect confidence.

Another long moment passed by before Nicholas finally lowered himself again to pepper sweet kisses across Dave's cheekbones and nose, mouth and chin. Then, close by Dave's ear, Nicholas tentatively asked, "Would you wear something?"

He pulled back again to see Dave's reaction. Dave frowned, not really knowing what to think. They usually had sex naked – and why not? Naked allowed for the complete experience, with no hindrances or frustrations or distractions. The only times they didn't get naked were when they were too frantic to bother completely undressing. Which wasn't a sex thing, but an urgency thing. So what did Nicholas mean? "Wear something … ?" Dave eventually echoed. "Like what?"

Nicholas flushed a little, which suggested a few horrible ideas to Dave.

"No, not like a … you want me to dress up as a …"

"Not necessarily."

"Or like a costume or something?"

Nicholas scrunched his face up. "I'm open to the possibilities, but that's not what I had in mind."

"Look," said Dave, struggling to sit up a bit and really face his lover. "I'm a man, all right? I know you fuck me a lot, and you usually do the driving in bed. But that doesn't make me –"

"Of course not!"

"I am *not* going to play the drag queen for you. I'm not a woman. I'm not going to pretend to be anything I'm not."

"That's *fine*, David," Nicholas said, starting to sound a bit exasperated.

Dave took a breath, and then sat up further against the headboard. Nicholas was kneeling between Dave's bent legs, but they weren't touching any more. Finally Dave managed, "Not that there's anything wrong with that for those who want to. But I don't. Want to."

"I get that," Nicholas remarked tartly. Then he softened a little. "For heaven's sake, David, I *like* that you're a man. You're all man even when you're getting fucked, I *promise*. And that totally works for me. I don't want to change anything about you."

"But you do, don't you? You want me to be gay, and I'm probably stuffing it up badly."

Nicholas groaned in frustration and annoyance. "I have news for you, David. All you have to do to be gay is love me. And actually you're pretty much a genius at that."

After another long moment of bullheadedness, Dave took a breath and tried to be more reasonable. "All right. Then, what is it you want me to do?"

"Nothing at all, if you don't want to – honestly."

"Yeah, *all right*, I trust you. Just tell me!" A silence stretched, and Dave belatedly reflected that no doubt Nicholas was now feeling as vulnerable and misunderstood as Dave himself had not a minute before. "Hey," Dave joshed. "You want me to wear a chauffeur's cap and call you sir? We can do that. Just don't … don't call me Frank in the middle of it, and we'll do fine."

Nicholas cast him a flat look. "I said it wasn't about costumes. And I so do not have a sense of humour about how I used to feel for Frank."

"Of course not," Dave offered softly. He sat forward, and let both his hands settle on Nicholas in a gentle caress. "Come on, tell me. If I can, I will, I promise. Even if I don't understand." That earned him a fond glance. "Be patient with me. I'm just a dumb Aussie who never had to think much about this sort of stuff. But I'm not a *totally* lost cause."

"No, that's the very last thing you are," Nicholas declared. Then he finally shifted forward so he was sitting with his legs curled under him, and one hand resting on Dave's thigh. Eventually he said, very quietly, "I like naked, I like skin. But I like silk, too. Would you wear something made of silk while we're in bed?" He dared to glance at Dave and then swiftly looked away. "Doesn't have to be feminine or anything. It's the … texture that counts. Not what it actually is."

Dave swallowed, not sure what he was really getting into. But he couldn't find anything to protest about in what Nicholas had just asked. "Well," he replied, both firmly and cautiously. "That sounds okay."

Nicholas shot him a grateful look – and then suddenly he was looking directly at Dave, directly *into* him, his gaze shockingly level and intent. Dave let out a breath that was almost a gasp, exactly as if Nicholas had just penetrated him. Nicholas drew closer – and Dave couldn't help but draw back, at least for an inch or two until his head collided *thunk* against the headboard.

"You know what I like best of all?" Nicholas asked.

Dave shook his head. No.

"I like looking into your eyes, your beautiful blue eyes, and they're so clear and you're so open to me, like an infinite sky, like a pool that sinks down *forever*. There are no barriers – not like there are at the moment. There's no confusion or doubt or pain or fear, there's just *you* … there's you letting me in … and me inside of you … there's just *us* together … and then there's the air and the sunlight and the pleasure, until at last – at last –"

"Oh God," said Dave roughly. "Silk or not, I don't care – just fuck me. Just fuck me now."

And that's what they did.

four

Denise called back a couple of days later, and chatted briefly with Dave before asking, "Who do I talk to about our clothes for the wedding, you or Nicholas?"

"Am I going to hate them?" Dave asked.

"No, you are *not* going to hate them!" she retorted in mock exasperation. "Don't you trust me any more, Davey?"

"Yeah, you know I do. Well, unless it's real simple and obvious, you'd better talk to him, right? Or I'll just confuse the issue when I pass it on."

"That's what I thought."

"Huh. Okay, hang on, and I'll get him for you. I'll just be a mo." Dave carefully put the phone down, and then jogged on through to the family living room where Nicholas was stretched out with a book.

Nicholas had been out of sorts from the moment Dave woke that morning, and Dave wasn't sure why – though he assumed it had something to do with the fact they were due to have lunch with a group of Nicholas's friends that day, most of whom were either former university friends or gay – or both. Dave himself was dreading it, and he imagined that Nicholas was, too.

Once Dave had conveyed what Denise wanted to talk about, Nicholas got an intent look on his face, and without saying a word in reply headed off to pick up the call. Dave figured he'd be better off leaving them to it, and settled on a sofa before taking up Nicholas's book and examining it. Which was about butterflies, of course, which meant that at least Dave could appreciate the pictures.

About fifteen minutes later, Nicholas came back into the room and stood looming over Dave with a thunderous scowl. "Did you tell her about the silk thing?" he demanded.

"No! What?" Dread fell through Dave and settled uneasily in his gut.

"Are you *sure*?"

"Of course I'm sure! I'm not gonna be talking sex stuff with Denise!" Which wasn't actually the point. The point was: "God. What does she want me to wear?"

Nicholas relaxed a fraction. "You'll like it. It's all right. A silk shirt and linen trousers. Maybe a waistcoat, too, silk or linen. You'll be fine."

Dave looked at him closely. Nicholas was still thoroughly out of sorts. "What about you?" Dave asked cautiously. "Are you okay with it?"

"Yes. Yes, I am." Nicholas at last folded down onto the sofa opposite Dave, and sat there hunched forward with his elbows on his knees. "You'll be smart–casual, while we'll be formal, but the colours will work together perfectly." He added with a humourless smile, "There's no point trying to dress you up as something you're not, is there?"

"No," Dave agreed, very quietly and very cautiously.

"Actually, I suspect Denise has just managed to rather creatively save the whole thing. I mean, it would have been good. Now it's going to be perfect."

"Well," said Dave, still rather cautious, "that's great. Isn't it?"

"Yes."

A silence threatened to drag out into something unbearable. "Look. Are you going to tell me what's bothering you? It's about me meeting your friends, isn't it? But, you know – I figure they'll be happy for you. Even if they don't like me."

"What?" Nicholas scowled again, this time looking honestly mystified. "Why on earth wouldn't they like you?"

"Because I barely made it through high school, and because I'm not, you know … gay enough."

"Oh, for God's sake, not *that* again."

"So," Dave retorted, "if that's not the problem, why don't you tell me what is, then?"

Nicholas stared at him as if Dave were a pinned butterfly that refused to be properly identified. "How would you describe yourself now? If asked. Gay? Straight? What?"

"See, I never had to think about it before. Because I had Denise."

"So why are you suddenly so keen on labels now, then?"

"I dunno. I guess because everyone else seems to be."

"Well … ?"

Dave let out a sigh. "Well, I suppose I'm … bi. Bisexual." He coloured up a bit. It was the first time he'd ever said the word aloud, and he had the horrible suspicion that some people would interpret bi as indecisive or maybe just lacking courage. "I mean, I loved Denise. That was real. But this is real, too. So I guess that makes me … both?"

"Exactly. And why the hell do you think my friends – whose business it so totally isn't, anyway – Why do you think they'd have any kind of problem with that?"

"I guess they wouldn't. But I just don't know how to … be."

"Fuck's sake! Just be yourself. You have no problem doing that when it comes to whether you'll wear a suit or not, do you?!"

Dave just stared back at the man, trying to scramble through all the confusion back to its source. "Um. Okay. So you think it's gonna go all right? Lunch, I mean."

Nicholas heaved an exasperated sigh. "Of *course* it is. Just what kind of idiotic friends do you think I have, anyway?" he added in a grumble.

A moment passed. "Right," said Dave. "So, what have you been unhappy about today? If it's not that."

Another moment passed while Nicholas just considered him, his annoyance at last dwindling away into something cooler. Eventually he said, "We have to go soon. There's not time to get into it. We'll talk about it later this afternoon, all right?"

"All right." Dave let out a breath, and made himself ask what Denise would have wanted him to ask if it were her. "Is it something – between us? Something I've done."

"No …" Nicholas gusted a breath and fell forward onto his knees, at last softening, warming, pushing into Dave's embrace. "No, not at all." They took each other into the deepest of hugs. "Nothing like that."

"You gonna give me a hint?"

"Just – I found another hoop. In the visa process."

"Ah, well. Hoops are for jumping through."

"And that's why you're the hero in the story of my life."

"Oh *Nicholas*," he groaned. And they held each other tightly there, prepared to deal together with all the world might throw at them.

The accord between them was wonderful, but it didn't last. Despite the fact that Nicholas's friends greeted Dave as if he were already their friend and had been all along – and despite the fact that Dave quickly relaxed in their company as if he'd just walked into a pub in Charleville rather than Beaconsfield – Nicholas was soon out of sorts again.

"I should have brought the Akubra," Nicholas grumbled. A table had been set for them outside in the beer garden along which ran a canal. There were willow trees on the other bank, and everything was idyllically English – but Nicholas grimaced fretfully up at the sunshine despite being under a broad canvas umbrella, and said, "I don't want to get too hot."

"Shall we see if we can move inside?" Dave asked – though they'd walked through the pub when they arrived, and it had been clear it was one of those really old places with rooms far too small and cramped to cope with even ten or twelve people all sitting together.

"No, it's all right."

"Drink, Nicholas?" someone asked.

"Still water with ice and lime," he said, squinting up at whoever it was. Dave hadn't managed to attach a single name to a face yet.

"David?" the someone continued. "I think they have Foster's on tap."

Dave suppressed a shudder, and decided the affronted lecture on what a Queenslander was prepared to drink could wait. "I'll have the same as Nicholas, thanks."

Nicholas looked at Dave, his expression scrunched up with concern now. "You can have a beer."

"I know. But I'll keep you company."

"Well. You might not want to start *that* habit. I should warn you I hardly ever drink."

"You drank beer in Australia," Dave remarked.

"Only ever one or two, not very often – and when in Rome …"

"You drink beer in Rome?"

"No! Idiot …" Nicholas guffawed with genuine humour, which made Dave smile. "I'm sorry," Nicholas said very quietly after a moment. "I'm just paranoid about getting headaches. Even … ordinary ones."

"I get it," Dave said, matching his tone. "D'you want to take a couple of your pain killers, just in case? Prevention being better than the cure."

Nicholas smiled at him fondly. "No, it's all right. I'll be all right."

"You go inside the moment you want to, and I'll get everyone else moved in as well, I promise. It won't be a problem."

The smile broadened, and Nicholas finally relaxed. "I like you looking after me."

"Just trying to return the favour," Dave asserted, endeavouring not to turn self–conscious and betray himself. When he finally turned away from Nicholas and sat back, he discovered that those people nearest him were regarding the pair of them very very fondly. It took every single ounce of his Aussie brashness to face them down – and even that didn't seem to dent their affection, not one little bit.

Late that afternoon Nicholas lay stretched out on their bed, unwinding and cooling down. They had all the windows open so the room was full of fresh air, and Nicholas lay there in just his jeans and a t–shirt. Dave sat beside him, up against the headboard, simply idling away the time. They weren't touching, for the sake of Nicholas not wanting any of Dave's body heat, but that didn't mean they weren't close.

Eventually, once Nicholas seemed to have reached something more like his usual happy demeanour, Dave asked, "D'you want to have a nap? I'll get out of your way, if you like."

"Maybe," said Nicholas, "and only if you want to."

"All right." After a moment, Dave said, "D'you want to tell me about the thing with the visa? If we get that sorted, then maybe you'll feel better."

A long quiet peace stretched, though it was clear to Dave that Nicholas hadn't slipped away into sleep. Eventually Nicholas said, "It's about my health. I guess I'd read it before, but it hadn't quite sunk in."

"What about it?"

"It's a serious condition, David. They're not going to like it. They might refuse me the visa."

Dave took a moment with that, then asked, "On what grounds? It's not like it's catching or anything. It's not like you're endangering anyone."

"No, it's about the fact that at some point – maybe not for years, decades – I'll probably need surgery. Brain surgery."

"So … ?"

Nicholas threw him a frustrated look. "It's the cost and resources involved. Why would they want to take me on? I can't even promise to pay my way in the meantime, unless I get really lucky with the right kind of work."

"Ah." Dave thought about all of that, though the answer seemed clear to him.

"I guess …" said Nicholas very slowly, "I could have the operation done here. Before we go."

"No!" cried Dave, his heart thudding painfully.

"But then it's not such an issue," Nicholas doggedly continued. "Of course, things could still go wrong later, but at least I'll have done what I can in the meantime."

"No," Dave firmly replied. "The risks aren't worth it. There's no point in you going through something so serious."

"There is a point if it means I can be with you."

Dave shifted down onto the bed and turned towards Nicholas. "I've got a much better idea, anyway."

Nicholas reached to take his hand. "What's that, then?"

"We don't rely on Medicare. That's like the NHS here – and that's where the cost to the government comes in, right?"

"Oh! Of course!"

"We'll take care of ourselves. We buy private health insurance, whatever it takes. It's not like we can't afford it – and then there's no financial risk involved to anyone else. Problem solved. Right?"

"Right," said Nicholas with a watery smile. "God, you're amazing!"

"Not too shabby, I guess."

"I just – I didn't think of that. Of course I already have health insurance as part of the family policy, and it covers me worldwide. I checked that before the trip. God! Why didn't I add that up myself?"

Dave smiled, and offered somewhat weakly, "Two heads are better than one."

"I am definitely better with you," Nicholas fervently replied – and he turned in against Dave, and Dave held him, cradled him for a while. Dave's shirt got suspiciously damp where Nicholas pressed his face against it, but then Nicholas finally drifted off into a restful sleep, and when he woke again he was his own best self.

Dave kind of adored Nicholas's blog entry for that day.

The Real Thing
It's true love. When Stef offered to buy David a Foster's at lunch today, David

refrained from violence and didn't even swear, but only politely replied that he'd have what I was having. All for the sake of not causing an irreconcilable rift with his new partner's old friends. It was remarkable.

Having quizzed David about the significance of all this, we decided that offering a Queenslander a Foster's was equivalent to putting Coca Cola in a Scot's whisky. So, you see how very remarkable this is …

True blue love, I tell you. Fair dinkum, mate.

five

'Yes, I'm all yours,' Dave had said to Nicholas on the first day he'd arrived in England – and in front of Nicholas's entire family as witnesses, not to mention their loyal retainers as well. There was many a time over the following weeks when Dave wished that had been all it took to be married. And of course in many ways – at least for the two of them – that had indeed been the moment in which they'd really committed themselves. That was never in question. Later on he'd followed that up with, *'For you, I'd even give up Australia.'* There was no doubt about Dave–and–Nicholas. The problem was all the other stuff that went on and inexorably on.

After the first couple of weeks which seemed plagued by upsets, Nicholas had – thank God – regained his equilibrium and dived into the wedding preparations with his usual cheerfulness. But he wanted the ceremony and reception to be absolutely perfect, which was pressure enough, never mind the business surrounding Nicholas's move to Australia and the visa requirements. Never mind him saying goodbye to his father and the rest of his family. And Nicholas had never been good at farewells.

One of the things Nicholas was good at was gifts. Within about a week and a half of Dave's arrival in England, Nicholas presented him with a new Kindle device on which was loaded all the Patrick O'Brian books. Given that Dave had only brought a couple of the paperbacks with him, he felt almost overwhelmed with gratitude. Jack Aubrey and Stephen Maturin had been his constant companions for so long, and their adventures provided inspiration or a failsafe refuge whenever needed. Right now, there was plenty to be doing and helping Nicholas with, and of course hanging out with Nicholas was always a good thing. But there was no denying that wedding plans and visa applications weren't quite as involving as planning and leading a trip in Australia's Outback. And there were times when Dave – so used to living on his own – needed an escape into the more solitary pleasures of reading.

As September turned into October, the level of activity in the house and its surrounds heightened. Mrs Gilchrist was responsible for the catering at the reception and was baking fruit cakes and accumulating crockery at an alarming rate; Frank was responsible for the cars they'd use and was also helping the head gardener add what seemed like hundreds of new plants to the flowerbeds so they looked as lush as possible; Simon was assisting Nicholas with the logistics. As the only surviving parent of either of them, Richard was taking his role as host – and as father or stand–in father of the grooms – with great gravity. New morning suits were being made and fitted by a tailor in Beaconsfield, but that was the province of Nicholas and Robert – apparently Dave and Nicholas weren't to see each other's outfits until the day of the wedding itself, despite Nicholas's nervousness about what Denise was organising for the Australian half of the wedding party.

"You can trust her," said Dave. "She knows far more about these things than I do. And I have to say she looked *great* when she married Vittorio." Denise in a simple elegant white wedding dress with her long blonde hair done up in a casual twist had been a revelation … Dave's heart had broken all over again.

"I have complete faith in her," Nicholas said – though his long pale fingers skittered away as if daring to disagree. "I loved her ideas. I honestly did."

"I believe you!" Dave asserted.

"Yes, I know," Nicholas replied rather miserably. "Thousands wouldn't."

Despite Dave not having any direct responsibilities other than being Nicholas's mainstay and willing assistant in all things, the stresses must have started to show. One evening, Richard happened upon Dave as he came down the main stairs into the hall, and took the opportunity to invite him into the study, the room where all the family photos were hanging on a wall. "Nothing to be alarmed about," Richard assured him as he took a seat in one of the leather armchairs – Dave had discovered that there were comfortable armchairs in just about every room in the house! The earl gestured an invitation for Dave to sit opposite him. "I was simply concerned for you, David."

"For me?" he blurted in surprise. "I'm all right."

Richard nodded as if genially agreeing. "You've been here a couple of months now, and I feel we've come to know something of you. David, it's clear that you're exactly the sort of fine, responsible young man any parent would wish for a son–in–law."

"Oh. Oh, well. Thanks." Dave was blushing again. Which was one thing he'd be glad to see the back of once he and Nicholas were married and it was all settled and accepted and *done*.

"I'm sorry to make you uncomfortable, but I want you to know how pleased and proud we all are."

"Thanks," said Dave again rather pathetically. He tried not to squirm.

Luckily Richard started talking about Nicholas instead. "Of course Nicholas is determined to live his life, and with good reason. He's an inspiration to us all, really. He sets the example for how to approach life."

"Yes."

"And we hope – we *fervently* hope – that it will all come to nothing, and Nicholas will outlive his own generation as well as mine."

"Yes," Dave agreed, though in rather muted tones.

"In the meantime, however, it's true that Nicholas … has a tendency to sweep all before him in his enthusiasms."

And Richard left a pause.

Eventually Dave offered, "But with what Nicholas is facing … I think seizing the day is the only answer. He's brave enough to do that."

"Yes, he's almost always faced this with courage – but he's been braver still since he met you, David. I was afraid he'd never quite let himself really love someone."

Dave couldn't possibly respond to that, but he stored it away for future comfort and somehow managed to sail blithely on. "It's like you said, seizing the day is something we should all do, really. Make the most of what time we have."

Richard nodded, but continued, "I am … only concerned, David, that you may have been swept up in something that you possibly now … regret."

"Regret?" he exclaimed, frowning at the man. "No, I'm not sorry about being with Nicholas. Are you?" he added, perhaps a bit too belligerently. "I mean, are you sorry I'm with him?" Dave clarified in more reasonable tones.

"Not at all – though we shall miss him a great deal when you're living on the other side of the world. We will miss both of you."

"I'm –"

Richard lifted a hand to stall whatever Dave had been going to say. "I realise that's what you both must do. No, what I was trying to say was that it's a significant burden to take on – a partner, a husband who might not live to see your first anniversary."

Dave swallowed hard at the thought, but of course he'd faced this already.

He'd faced it for Nicholas, and he'd faced it in all kinds of other ways, too. "We all live with that, though, don't we?" he said. "Like you said, Nicholas might outlive me. If he doesn't – Well, my mother died when I was young, and my father not so long ago. Any trip I take into the Outback might be my last, no matter how careful I am. We all live with death, Richard. Nicholas already knows what the only answer to that is. Sometimes I – Well, there have been times I needed to be reminded of that." He took a breath, and firmly concluded, "I don't have any regrets, Richard. I'm grateful. With Nicholas around, I'm never going to forget again – I'll never forget to *live*."

It seemed that Richard was moved, and he needed a long moment before he could be sure of his voice. Eventually he said, very very lightly, "I once asked Nicholas how he knew you were the man for him. Do you know what he said?"

"No. Actually, I don't." Dave cringed a little inside, just in case.

"He said that right from the day you first met, he felt utterly *safe* with you."

"Oh." That wasn't so bad. Dave relaxed again.

"He added that maybe I'd been hoping for a more passionate answer."

"No, actually that's kind of perfect, isn't it?"

"Yes, David," the earl replied with great warmth, "actually it kind of is."

His Imagination

David apologises for reading – as if I could possibly mind. He says he feels bad for ignoring me, sometimes for hours at a stretch. He doesn't seem to realise I love him all the more for being a reader. Our best selves are readers.

And look what he has chosen for his other world! Books as clever and clear–eyed as they are kind and courageous. Who wouldn't fall for a man who shares his imagination with Jack Aubrey and Stephen Maturin?

At last it was mid–October, and Denise was due to arrive at Heathrow early one morning. She and Dave had of course spent time apart before, but never for so long, and never with half a world between them. He didn't expect her to have missed him as much as he'd missed her, but still. Dave anticipated a damp–eyed reunion in the grand tradition of airline ads everywhere. And of course it wasn't only Denise, but Charlie, and Zoe, and Vittorio.

Dave and Nicholas were up at five, and on their way by half past. Dave was driving Robert's Renault Espace, which had room for everyone. Frank had fitted a baby seat for Zoe. There was almost no traffic at that time of the morning, of course, so they made it there in about twenty minutes – and then it was a matter of Dave anxiously waiting by the barriers, while Nicholas went to fetch them coffee.

At last Dave's disparate little family appeared, and he beamed like an idiot as they saw him and headed in his direction, all of them obviously tired and a bit frumpy, but all of them just as obviously happy. Soon Dave and Denise were holding onto each other tight, as if they were two halves of a whole that had been too long sundered. Then wonderful Charlie must have a great warm hug, too – and then even Vittorio claimed one – and Zoe, who was strapped to her father in a carrier, lifted her hands and yearned towards Dave as if she might even remember him. "She's, like, doubled in size again!" Dave exclaimed, quite astounded by the changes. He was ashamed to realise he wasn't quite sure if he'd have recognised her.

"She's thriving," Denise said, quite complacently. "Though she'll be all the better for seeing you again, Davey."

"I'm all the better for it, too."

Before Dave could completely let the side down with sentiment in excess of the standard Aussie limits, Vittorio got them all moving towards the exit, with him and Charlie pushing the trolleys of luggage, and Nicholas leading them to the car park. Soon they were on their way back to the Goring family home, and the sun was rising into what promised to be a perfect English day. Denise sat up the front with Dave, catching him up on all the Brisbane gossip, while Charlie sat in the back with Nicholas, and Vittorio took care of Zoe.

Then they were home, and Simon and Frank were helping with the bags, and Richard was there to welcome everyone and show them to their rooms, and invite them to come back down for breakfast as soon as they'd settled in and freshened up. All was glorious chaos for a long while, except that in the midst of it, Dave got to sit at the breakfast table holding Zoe and feeding her, and the two of them gazed at each solemnly, and remembered anything about each other that they might have forgotten.

There was a quiet half hour with Denise late that morning as well, as she showed him the clothes she'd had made for the two of them for the wedding, and for Charlie as well – and she also had some news. "I'm pregnant again, Davey. So, if you're up for another irreligious godchild …"

"Always," he vowed. "Me and Nicholas maybe? As godparents?"

"Yes, absolutely. You and Nicholas. For Zoe, too." Denise laughed fondly, and whispered, "But mostly you, Davey."

He reached instinctively to rest a reverential hand against her stomach – and thought better of it just in time. But Denise took his hand and held it against her warm belly, still flat yet full of possibilities. "I've missed you, you know."

"It won't be long now, and I'll be home again."

"And your man with you, where he belongs."

Dave grinned at her, no doubt a bit lopsidedly. "Where we both belong, yes."

Denise turned away, busying herself with the unpacking. But she quieted after a moment, and said, "You're still sure about this, are you? Getting hitched, I mean."

"Yes. Why?"

"It's all happened pretty quick, that's all."

"It was quick for you and Vittorio, too. You just know, don't you? You know when it's worth trying, anyway."

"Yes."

"And this whole 'Seize the Day' philosophy has a lot going for it."

Denise laughed a little under her breath, and shot him a glance. Apparently if she'd really had any worries, he'd just convinced her as easily as that.

He watched as Denise carefully hung up the wedding clothes in one of the wardrobes, and then he dared to say – now while they were still a bit punch drunk with jet lag or the reunion or the early start to the day. He dared to say, "Nicholas has this thing, you know …"

"So I gathered."

"Ha ha." And he was blushing already. Dave sighed, and continued anyway because he knew Denise wouldn't let him get away with changing the subject now. "He asked me if … if I'd wear something silk. To bed. And I guess he wasn't talking pyjamas."

Denise came and sat beside him, and considered him seriously. "What d'you think about that?" she asked.

He shrugged. "I'm not meant to tell you. In fact, I said I wouldn't. He was – When you talked to him about the silk shirt for the wedding, he was mad at me, cos he thought I'd told you."

"So why are you telling me now?"

"I want you to help me. You did good with the wedding clothes. I figured you could help me with this."

Denise reached to grasp his hand for a moment, and then let him go before asking very matter–of–factly, "Are we talking lingerie? Something a woman would wear?"

Dave's face was waratah red, he could feel it, but he pushed on. He could trust Denise, and he wanted to make Nicholas happy. "I don't know. He said it didn't have to feminine, he just liked silk. But then he said actually that didn't matter, and he started talking about how he likes it best when I'm – um … When there's no barriers, yeah? Does that make sense? When it's just him and me …" He gestured, helplessly, with both hands miming the gates over his heart opening – and then flitting to and fro between their mutually engaged gazes.

"Davey –"

"Mmm?"

"He's not into … humiliating you. Is he?"

"No! God, no, nothing like that."

"You trust him?"

"*Totally.*"

"He wants to … really *experience* that, I guess."

"Yeah, I guess so. And it's good, you know? When it's intense like that." Dave looked at her. "I need your help, Denny. I need you to figure out what I could wear – I mean, what it would take – to go far enough for him – and not too far for me."

"If you really trust him," she said very carefully, "then what would be too far?"

"Well, you know. If I just ended up feeling ridiculous. Would be kinda counter–productive. Don't you think?"

"Yeah, I get it." She frowned over all of this for a long moment with her head down, and then reached to hold his hand again. "No worries, mate," Denise said softly, her gaze meeting his with no judgement. "No worries.

We'll figure it out."

And Dave let out a breath he'd barely known he'd been holding.

On the following Saturday night, Robert and Penelope took Denise and Vittorio out for dinner, and left Nicholas and Dave at home to celebrate a joint buck's night – not only with Charlie, but also with Zoe and Robin and all the other Goring children. They took over the family lounge room and played games, watched *Monsters, Inc.* and generally had a wonderful time. Nicholas read aloud from a Roald Dahl book chosen by Robin, and Charlie told a Dreamtime story that had all the kids enraptured – and the adults, too.

Dave thought the whole thing was hilarious. "I never thought I'd be over-indulging in *ice cream* on my buck's night!" But it was also completely perfect. "Best night ever," he quietly commented as he accompanied Nicholas carrying a sleepy Robin up to his bedroom once all the other kids had finally been reclaimed by their parents.

"Best ever …" Robin echoed. "Love you, Nic'las."

"Love you, too, my darling boy."

And Robin clung on with his arms around Nicholas's neck, and had to be gently prised off before at last he curled up on his own in his bed and fell heavily into sleep.

Dave knew just how the young fellow felt – though he realised now that unlike Robin he'd never once declared himself. He'd never used the L word to Nicholas. Though perhaps at this point he didn't really need to. Dave figured maybe it was understood.

It seemed that no decision relating to the wedding could possibly be straightforward. There was probably some kind of law about it. The current topic was cars. As there were only five people attending the actual ceremony – Nicholas and Dave, Robert and Denise, and Richard – Robert's idea was that they would all just go in one car and he would drive. Richard, however, thought that Nicholas and Dave should have a little time alone together after the ceremony, and therefore they should travel home separately, and Simon could drive them. Robert seemed to find this a bit unnecessary, though he didn't seem to have any particular reason why. Nicholas seemed to like the idea, but was concerned about Simon already having enough to do that day with organising the reception and helping Penelope to welcome the guests.

Robert and Richard were amicably arguing the matter back and forth between them when Dave noticed that Robin had sidled up to Nicholas and was whispering in his ear. When Nicholas pulled back a little to consider him, Dave could see that Robin was upset about something.

Nicholas made up his mind and settled the dispute. "It'll have to be two cars," he announced, "because Robin's coming, too." On which Robin clung to him, and Nicholas hauled the young fellow up onto his lap for a cuddle.

"Would there be room for Charlie as well, then?" Dave asked.

Robert still seemed a bit disgruntled over something, but everyone agreed that yes, there'd certainly be room for Charlie. And so that, at least, was finally sorted.

six

Early on the morning of the thirty–first of October, Dave woke nestled deep in the bed, with Nicholas curled around him pressing sleepy kisses to his nape. "Good morning, husband," Nicholas murmured with his lips brushing against Dave's skin.

Dave shivered in delight – and snorted. "Not yet, I'm not!"

"Mmm … Our last chance for a bit of illicit fornication …"

"You don't want to save yourself … ?"

"At least a decade too late for that!"

"Tart!"

"And you can't resist a fine tasty tart."

"That's true."

So they made love, just as they were, still warm and blurred with sleep, Nicholas thrusting gently against Dave's rear and each with a hand overlapping on Dave's cock echoing the same sweet rhythm. They spilled over with sighs, and still wrapped up close they snoozed again for a few minutes, before at last the alarm went off.

"Good morning, husband," Nicholas said again.

Dave chuckled. "Come on, then. Let's make that happen!"

They each had a quick shower and dragged on the nearest casual clothes, then headed down to join the rest of the family for breakfast. The general mood was cheerful yet busy. Everyone made a point of greeting Dave and Nicholas, and wishing them well.

Dave found that he wasn't very hungry, so after he'd drunk his coffee he made his excuses and wandered outside for some fresh air. He must have been looking pensive, for when Simon popped his head out of the front door to find Dave pacing back and forth on the driveway, he asked, "The not unexpected cold feet, sir, or is it serious second thoughts?"

He managed a low chuckle in reply. "Neither, really. And today of all days, you can call me Dave, can't you?"

Simon came out to join him in the cool morning air, closing the door behind him. "We're a bit more formal here in England than you're used to, I imagine."

"Just a bit," he replied, bunging on the irony.

"You know, … Dave. You must always ask if you need anything."

"Thanks, Simon," he said with a nod. "I will. And – likewise."

"I mean, sir, that I would consider myself to be serving the ultimate good of the family, if there was something you wanted … even if you felt they wouldn't agree. I would be happy to serve you, sir."

Dave eyed him narrowly. "Are you encouraging me to make a run for it?"

"Not encouraging, Mr Taylor. Merely making sure that you know it's a possible course of action. If you wish to take it."

"I don't. But I appreciate the thought." They paced back and forth together companionably for a while, before Dave confessed, "I've been thinking that I've never said – those three little words to him."

"I am sure that Nicholas is very much aware of how you feel for him. We can all see it."

"Yeah? Then why do people keep asking me if I want to get out of this?"

"Ah." Simon considered the gravel at his feet for a moment. "Nicholas does have a way of carrying all before him. Everyone here loves him dearly, and he's too sensitive a man to deliberately hurt anyone. We have, however, learned to speak up on the few occasions when we've needed to." Simon tipped his head towards Dave. "I suppose there might be some concern that you have yet to learn that."

"No, that's all right. I can fend for myself. Australians are rarely backward in coming forward."

"Of course, sir. Dave. Well, if I may, I would like to wish you every joy today and in all the days to come."

"Thank you, Simon. You, too, mate." And Dave went back inside and drank another coffee.

Soon it was time for Dave to head off with Denise and their little family to get formally dressed. Nicholas kissed him on parting, and told Dave how beautiful he was going to be. Treating him just like a bride! "God, shut up," Dave grumbled. "Anyway, you know no one's gonna outshine you."

Nicholas chortled in surprise. "Oh, I do believe you have it bad, Mr Taylor."

"I do, sir," he murmured in reply. "I have it very bad indeed …"

And they were parted, not to meet again until they were suited and groomed, and ready for the ceremony.

Dave got dressed in Charlie's room, under Denise's supervision. She was stunning in a dress of heavy silk that looked as if it had simply been draped snugly around her figure but might slip off again at any moment. It was coloured the grey–green of eucalyptus leaves. She'd had a shirt made for Dave in the same material, along with dark grey linen trousers with a slightly rough weave.

There was also a silk waistcoat of a hazy dark green–blue. It was a simple design, without any collar and with rather discreet buttons, but it was nicely fitted – and a step or two more formal than Dave was really comfortable with.

"You don't have to wear that," said Denise. "Just the shirt, trousers and proper shoes are enough."

"Nicholas would like it, though," Dave responded. "Wouldn't he?"

"Yes, I think so."

"Okay, then." Dave had had his way about the morning suits, after all, so he could make a gesture in return.

Charlie, meanwhile, was dressed in the same kind of trousers, and a shirt of the same silk but coloured a dusky version of pink eucalyptus flowers. He looked absolutely magnificent.

"Jeez …" Dave complained. "Just as I'd gotten used to being the centre of attention for once, you two decide to go and look, like, *ten* times more gorgeous than me!"

"As if," Denise returned.

"And it's *my* wedding day, thank you very much!"

"Don't worry about it, mate," Charlie said with some fervour. "You look about as beautiful as a white fella can."

Which made Dave turn about as pink as Charlie's shirt – and then he went red as Denise pressed a kiss to his cheek that was warmer than any she'd bestowed on him since they'd broken up.

And maybe she'd done that deliberately, for he didn't manage to raise a protest as she fixed a buttonhole corsage to his waistcoat. It was made of creamy–white eucalyptus flowers and leaves. "How d'you manage that?" he asked in a subdued kind of voice.

"They're silk," she replied.

And there it was again: silk. Dave sat down on the nearest chair, and tried very hard to pretend that he didn't feel rather dizzy.

Charlie was shrugging into a grey–green silk waistcoat, which unfortunately toned down the effect of the pink, but it did turn them into a proper coordinated wedding party. Dave shook his head, thinking that Denise had worked some kind of miracle – and praying that Nicholas recognised it as such. There was a buttonhole corsage for Charlie, and then a silk shawl and a wrist corsage for Denise – all in pinks. And they were done.

Denise was considering the three of them with pride. "Not too shabby for a bunch of colonials, if I do say so myself!"

"It's marvellous, Denny," Dave said.

Charlie was beaming happily. And then Vittorio came in with Zoe wrapped in a carrier across his chest, and told everyone how wonderful they looked – though it was true his gaze lingered longest on his wife. Which was as it should be, Dave figured.

"They're bringing the cars around now," Vittorio continued. "Nicholas said he'll be away in about five minutes, and then if you follow when you're ready."

"This is it, then, Davey," said Denise.

He had to clear his throat before he could speak, but that was just the expected jitters. "I'm ready," Dave said. "I'm ready now."

Simon drove Dave, Denise and Charlie to Beaconsfield in the Rolls Royce Silver Cloud. When they got to the old courthouse and parked behind Robert's Renault Espace, Dave was amused and touched to find Frank there in his full chauffeur uniform, despite the fact that he knew Robert had done the driving. Apparently Frank felt the need to also give Nicholas away, or shine up the cars, be available to deal with any breakdowns, or some such thing. Dave went to shake his hand, and received a solemn nod in return.

Then Dave headed inside with two of his very best friends at his shoulders. His third best friend gaped in wonder for a moment on seeing him – and then beamed more brightly than he'd ever smiled before. Nicholas strode across the lobby to meet Dave, and to take both of Dave's hands in his own. "God, David – you look – you look *beautiful* …"

"So do you," he offered perfectly genuinely. Nicholas wore a grey morning suit as if it had been designed for him, for his tall, lovely figure with his slim waist and strong shoulders. There was a creamy–white rosebud on his lapel, and under the grey suit was a sage–green waistcoat, an ivory shirt, and a dusky–rose cravat. Dave was grinning at his husband–to–be for the sheer delight of seeing him, but he was also beginning to see that between them Nicholas and Denise had come up with a genius solution to the clothes problem. The away team were certainly far more casually dressed than the home team, but the shades of grey, pink and green – while very Australian on one hand and very English on the other – made the whole thing work together perfectly. "God, this is brilliant!" Dave exclaimed.

"Denise," said Nicholas in heartfelt tones – though he didn't let Dave go. "Thank you. *Thank you.*"

She was happy, too. "My pleasure, Nicholas."

"And as for you, Charles," Nicholas continued. "How gorgeous are you in pink! You almost make me wish I hadn't seen David first."

Charlie guffawed under his breath. Richard and Robert had come over by then, and each shook Charlie's hand, and kissed Denise on the cheek, with much murmured admiration. Robin was standing there looking somewhat overawed by the whole thing – and also utterly charming in a perfectly tailored morning suit of his own.

Dave, who'd been dreading so many aspects of this day, found himself declaring, "I can hardly even wait to see the photos!"

Nicholas laughed. "Hey, let's get married first, though, eh? Seeing as we're here."

"Yes, let's," Dave agreed. And they turned, and walked together hand–in–hand into the Disraeli Room and down the aisle, with their beloved friends and family following along behind.

"I declare that I know of no legal reason why we may not register as each other's civil partner. I understand that in signing this document we will be forming a civil partnership with each other."

Those were the formal vows, such as they were. Even Dave thought they lacked poetry. But then they each said a few words of their own, and they exchanged rings.

Nicholas said: "From the first day I met you, David, you made me feel safe. You made me realise that I could unfurl my wings and be myself and simply live. I'm not afraid any more. I'm not afraid. No matter how long or short a time we have together, I want you to know – I want you to always remember – that no one has ever been happier than how I am with you. David, I want to spend the rest of my life with you."

And Dave replied, "Then that's what we'll do."

Dave said: "We were friends first. Even though I turned you down, and it took me ages to realise what we could be together, you were a real friend to me, and I was a friend to you. We took care of each other, right from the start. And we still have that, that's still the bedrock, even though we have so much more as well now. We take care of each other, and we'll go on looking after each other for all the years to come. And that means the world to me. Nicholas, I want to spend the rest of my life with you."

And Nicholas replied, "Then that's what we'll do."

Everyone was so happy, and the whole thing felt so charged. Robin finished off the ceremony by reading out a poem by A.A. Milne called *Us Two*. Dave had originally thought Winnie–the–Pooh a rather bizarre choice for a wedding ceremony, but hearing it on the day, when they were already bubbling over with joy, he felt it was absurdly apt.

Even then, though, he wasn't quite done because there was something more he had to say – now, for the record, and with witnesses. Just as the registrar was about to call time, Dave said for them all to hear, "I love you, Nicholas. I *love* you."

And Nicholas said, "I love you, too, David Taylor."

And they were married.

honeymoon

seven

Dave and Nicholas spent their wedding night in an old manor house turned hotel about a half–hour drive from the Goring family home. Their room was large and seemed to date back centuries. It was all rich worn reds and wood panelling, tapestries and velvets, with an enormous four–poster bed. The en suite bathroom seemed to date back no later than yesterday, though the style of it all was old–fashioned.

Dave didn't take much of this in, however. They were both quiet, and only had eyes for each other, though Dave was growing more and more bashful at the thought of what was ahead, while Nicholas seemed to be calmer and more confident by the moment. They ate a very light supper in the hotel restaurant – both drinking plenty of water with lime juice, which seemed to be becoming a firm habit despite all the teasing about Dave being at risk of forfeiting his Australian citizenship.

Soon it was time to head upstairs.

The room was dark and mysterious now, with only a bedside lamp glowing and a wood fire burning in the large fireplace, throwing light and making the shadows dance. Dave wandered in, feeling a little lost, while Nicholas locked the door securely behind them.

Then Nicholas was there before him, taking his hands, and pressing a gentle kiss to Dave's mouth. "I thought I'd go and have a shower. Or do you want to go first? I want to be – perfect for you."

"You go first," Dave managed to whisper.

Another kiss, and then Nicholas headed off, humming to himself quite happily.

Dave sorted through the gear in his overnight bag, and then just sat on a chair and waited. It felt like forever and like not long enough, but then Nicholas reappeared, damp and flushed and dressed only in his favourite blue robe. "Your turn," Nicholas said brightly.

Dave grabbed his gear, and headed for the bathroom without a word.

He said 'I love you' today. Is it weird that we hadn't said that before? It's not like we didn't know. If there were any doubts, then him coming to England pretty much put those to rest.

We got married today, and he said 'I love you'.

He's in the shower now, and when he comes out —

Well. I have so much to write about, what with the ceremony and the reception. So many photos to share. Our wonderful family and friends. Thank you. If you were a part of today, and you're reading this: Thank you. It was astonishing.

But I think I'll keep this post short. I am just about to have better things to do …

He said 'I love you'.

Dave took somewhat longer getting ready than Nicholas, though eventually even Dave got impatient with himself, and he cautiously opened the door and stepped through into the bedroom.

Nicholas was waiting for him, sitting on the side of the bed. A lovely smile dawned on Nicholas's face as he took in the sight of Dave's new cream silk robe. Dave just stood there, pinned by Nicholas's gaze. After a moment, Nicholas asked in quietly appreciative tones, "Is that silk you're wearing for me … ?"

Yes. He couldn't find his voice, so he just nodded. He knew his cheeks were glowing pink, and not from the heat of the shower.

"Come here, you gorgeous thing …"

He walked a little closer and then tilted his head away, not wanting to refuse. But wanting to get this over with. He took a breath, and then lifted a hand to the robe's belt; pulled at one end, and let the knot fall away. The robe sighed open, and revealed what he wore underneath.

Nicholas gasped, and fell to his knees on the floor, staring.

It was only a plain slip in the same cream silk, though shaped – on the bias, Denise said – to be slightly snugger around his waist. It wasn't much, but it was enough to make Dave feel exquisitely self–conscious.

"Oh, *David* …" Nicholas lifted reverential hands to shape around the front of Dave's thighs. Staring. Still staring.

Dave wasn't quite sure how much Nicholas could see, but the slip was barely long enough, and he thought his cock must be peeking out below the silk hem. He felt more naked than naked.

He let the robe slip back off his shoulders and down his arms while Nicholas watched, and then he let it go so it slid right down and pooled on the floor about his feet.

"You are so very beautiful," Nicholas said in hushed tones. He pressed his face in against Dave's cock and balls, caressing them through the silk, his hands slipping around to Dave's rear.

When Nicholas sat back on his heels again and looked up, Dave offered the gold silk ribbons he'd held clutched in one hand. "I didn't know –"

"Oh, my darling man …" Nicholas pressed a kiss to Dave's hand and took the ribbons – after a moment he tied one around Dave's right thigh, about midway down, finishing it off with a bow. He pressed a kiss just above it. "All right?" he asked.

Dave nodded. He felt … adorned. He felt as if he were worth adorning. Worth adoring. Such a notion had hardly even entered his head before.

Nicholas took another ribbon, and tied it around Dave's left wrist, taking up the long ends and tying bow after bow with them until the ribbon became a golden corsage. Then Nicholas put the other ribbons aside, and simply spent forever and forever suckling at Dave's balls and rubbing his nose at the base of Dave's cock until it stood proud, jutting out from under the silk – until Dave himself only remained upright in the warm haze of pleasure because of Nicholas's hands firmly holding onto his hips, and his own hands resting on Nicholas's shoulders.

"Come to the bed," Nicholas eventually said. He stood, bringing the ribbons with him, and he led the way despite it only being a few steps. He climbed up onto the sheets, kneeling there and carefully bringing Dave after him, carefully laying him down, arranging him there on his back with his knees bent. Nicholas showed Dave the ribbons. "I'll tie you down, if you like – or you could promise me not to move unless I say so."

"I promise," said Dave, his voice as rough as if he hadn't used it all day. He wasn't sure it was a promise he could keep, but he was already dealing with enough without being bound as well. "I promise I'll try."

"Good," said Nicholas. "That's so good. I love you so much …"

"I love you, too," he replied. And he watched as Nicholas arranged him, he watched Nicholas and let himself be arranged. His feet were slid up close to his butt, and his knees gently pressed as wide apart as they would go. His arms were stretched out to each side. There was nothing for his hands to hang onto, but he figured he could cope with that, he could keep them there.

Nicholas knelt between Dave's spread thighs, and slid his hands around Dave's waist; grasped him either side just above his hipbones, and gently encouraged him upwards. "Come on … arch your back the way you like to."

He did – happily, obediently – feeling that delicious curve shaping his backbone, feeling his thighs widen further still, his head tilt back and press into the pillow. He felt glorious, and then there was the silk shifting against his skin – Nicholas had been so right about that – and the ribbons adorning him, Nicholas adoring him …

"Now, stay exactly there, my darling man …" And Nicholas bent to take Dave's cockhead into his mouth, and suckle as sweetly as he'd treated Dave's balls; it was the only contact between them, and it held something of the divine.

Dave moaned raggedly, loving the feel of Nicholas's mouth on him with no barriers, no protection. They'd had the tests done weeks ago, but then with nothing being said, they'd taken a step back, somehow agreeing to save this experience for this night, to help make it all really count. Which meant that soon – soon – not soon enough – Nicholas would be fucking him for the first time without a rubber, there'd be Nicholas and Dave and nothing between them. Dave groaned in need, and arched up just a little more, opened his thighs, opened himself a little more, pushing the boundaries a little further. Nicholas chuckled around his cock, and the tremors made Dave *shake* …

Then a well–lubed finger slid into him and he was lost … lost … lost in warm golden darkness and a pleasure so intense. He tossed his head and a moan reverberated through him. He wasn't sure – he'd meant to ask, but he had no words – he wasn't sure if he was allowed to come yet – but the pleasure went on forever, for impossibly ever – and with no warning the end was upon him, and Nicholas rumbled appreciatively around him which meant it was permitted, it was approved – and the pleasure surged through him, making him quake so that even though he grabbed at the sheets with either hand, he couldn't help himself, he shook loose and lost the pattern he was meant to keep – his feet planted firmly and his thighs pushed him up – but that was all right, for Nicholas was holding onto his hip with one strong hand, staying with him, Nicholas's mouth and finger drawing every last ounce of pleasure through him and then returning it tenfold.

"Oh …" he groaned, collapsing back at last, sprawling back … "sorry, I'm sorry …"

"You beautiful man," Nicholas said fervent and low. "God, you're incredible, you taste like the purest nectar. No wonder the butterflies couldn't get enough!" Then he was kneeling up between Dave's thighs, pushing in close and hauling Dave's rear onto his own thighs – intent – but not so intent that he didn't take care to ask, "All right? David?"

"Please," he said. "Please."

Dave's legs were too heavy with satiation to move, but Nicholas lifted one to hook a heel on his shoulder, bent the other leg around his waist – and then was pushing in, his cock lubed and *hot* and hard and it was so fucking intense, so fucking good – Dave cried out as if sundered, his eyes closing, his hands clutching, but Nicholas was wise enough to hear that right, to read that, to know that Dave was feeling it and *loving* it. And Dave gasped, and opened his eyes, opened himself further, let Nicholas's gaze pour down into him, and fill him, so they were two made one.

And they didn't last long, how could they possibly last – Nicholas's guttural groans rolling through them both, his long pale fingers digging into Dave's flesh as if hanging on for life itself – and then Nicholas was crying out and coming, his seed pulsing deep within Dave, a wet blessing deep inside him, Nicholas's seed becoming a part of him now – and the pleasure impossibly surged through Dave again, just once in an aftershock, leaving him weak and dazed and wonderful –

At last Nicholas collapsed down beside him, and they managed to shift, to hold each other near, Nicholas peppering kisses to whatever of Dave he could reach, until eventually the giddiness ebbed away and they both quietened, and then slipped away into a peaceful doze.

eight

Their wedding night had been spent in the luxuries of the best room in a manor house; their honeymoon would be spent in an isolated cottage on the Lizard Peninsula of Cornwall. Not that they were exactly roughing it, as the cottage belonged to a friend of Robert's and had been done up in a suitably traditional style but with no expense or mod–con spared. Also, Dave had to laugh at the English definition of 'isolated', as the village of Lizard was no further away than a ten– or fifteen–minute stroll.

Still, they had a magnificent view all to themselves, with the only other human construction in sight an old circle of standing stones on top of a steep rise to the north of them. Otherwise there was grassy moorland, with a sheltering hill close behind them, and in front – to the west – nothing but the edge of a high cliff, with the ground to the north descending to craggy rocks, then continuing on until eventually curving round to the west. Beyond all of that was the ocean. The beautiful, powerful ocean stretching all the way to a distant horizon. The place was quite breath–taking.

"Stunning," was Nicholas's muttered verdict on their first evening there as the sun began westering. "Stunning." He was, unnervingly, loitering almost right on the cliff edge, and with his hands jammed in his jeans pockets, too, so he wouldn't be able to grab onto anything if he tripped over his own clumsy feet or lost his balance.

"Mate," said Dave, easing up near him – though not too near. "Come back here, would you? I am *not* going to lose you when we've only been married a day. And especially not over a cliff. It would make me seem – a bit too laid–back."

"But take a look down here! It's like we've got our own little private beach."

First Dave had heard of it. He sidled a little closer, and carefully peered over. A long way down – a *long* way down at the foot of the cliff, there was a crescent of pure white sand between two sharp dark outcrops of rock, with gorgeous turquoise water lapping gently on this mild day. "Beautiful," he said. And he'd thought Australia had cornered the market on beautiful beaches. But then he looked at the surrounds, which were mostly sheer cliffs. "We're never getting down there, though. I don't know if you'd even want to land a boat. They have pretty high tides here, don't they?"

"Not as high as South Wales, but two or three metres on a regular basis."

"And all those rocks," Dave continued, figuring he'd better quash any of Nicholas's whimsies before they turned into wants. "Not the place to go taking chances in boats."

"No," Nicholas agreed. "This area is known for its shipwrecks. All the 'romance' of the high seas!"

"Right. Not exactly the sort of romance we're after just now." Dave turned away, and looked for alternatives. "We could go explore those standing stones."

Nicholas obligingly came away from the cliff edge, but cast him a wry look. "Now who's being reckless … ?"

"Reckless?" Dave considered the stones, which had obviously been standing there for hundreds if not thousands of years. "Well, you'd be pretty unlucky if one of them happened to fall on you, after all this time."

Nicholas laughed, but followed along as Dave started ambling in that direction. "Where's your imagination, David Taylor? You – maybe one day the custodian of a Dreamtime site!"

"Oh." All right, that had probably been pretty stupid. "I don't know anything about standing stones. I guess they're full of religious significance, then?"

"We don't know. They were made so long ago that their purpose has been forgotten. The knowledge hasn't survived like it has for the Aborigines in Australia. All we have are theories. And superstitions."

That didn't sound like so much fun. Not that Dave really believed in any of that kind of stuff, but here they were, alone in an isolated cottage with nothing but a circle of standing stones for company. And a very high cliff just beyond their front door. Dave was beginning to wonder if it would actually be a very good idea to spend the entire honeymoon in bed. He was just about to suggest this notion, when Nicholas continued, "There's probably a ghost story or two about these stones. We should ask around."

"Or not," said Dave. "Don't you think it's better not to know? Then we can just admire them as … as a feat of engineering. Something kinda beautiful, created by people who were probably every bit as smart as us. Or most of us, anyway … Certainly a lot cleverer than me!"

They were almost at the stones, and both remained silent for the last short climb up the steep rise. Then they were in the circle – what must have been at one time a pretty much perfect circle of tall stones, a total of –

"Don't count them!" blurted Nicholas.

"What?" Dave scowled at him. "Too late, anyway. There's –"

"*No!* Don't tell me!"

"Oh, for God's sake …" Dave rolled his eyes, while Nicholas either looked at Dave directly or at their general surroundings rather indirectly as if not even letting his subconscious pick up the pattern. "Right." There were nine stones in the circle, with their surfaces worn but most of them standing true, and only one looking as if it had been broken off at some stage. Then there was a tenth stone, squarer than the others and lying flat in the centre. There was a margin of bare dirt around the latter, as if the grass had been worn away by visiting feet. Dave wandered up to it, and propped his own foot on one edge. "So, what was this for, then?"

Nicholas shrugged. "We tend to think of them as altars, and I suppose they probably were. That's where some of the stories come in, anyway. People were sacrificed or executed or murdered on that, and their ghosts remain to haunt us."

Dave squinted at his partner, who was standing there with his hands shoved in his pockets and his shoulders hunched as if his hackles were up. "D'you believe in ghosts, then?" Dave asked, trying not to sound quite as sceptical as he actually was. "I thought you were a scientist!"

"I don't know … Not really …"

"You *do*, don't you!"

"Well, everything's made of matter and energy. *We're* made of matter and energy. When we die, where does that energy go? If it's a good death, a peaceful death, maybe it just … transforms into other, entirely natural forces. If not …" And Nicholas actually shivered. "If not, maybe it lingers."

Dave considered him for a long moment, then walked back over to him and ran a hand down the underside of his bare forearm. "You know what?"

"What?" Nicholas looked at him, unsmiling.

"This is our honeymoon, remember? I reckon we should just head back to the cottage, and get settled in. And then we can climb into bed, and seriously try spending the entire two weeks there."

That earned him a grin, though Nicholas still seemed a bit shaky. "Sounds like a plan."

"It *is* a plan. Nothing and nobody is going to bother us there. Everyone knows a blanket will protect you against anything, ghosts or otherwise."

Nicholas laughed. They had already left the stone circle, and were ambling back down the hill. "Will you let me have one afternoon out of bed, though? Just one?"

"Dunno. Depends."

"I just want to –" Nicholas looked about him. "The coastal path must run round the back of the hill behind the cottage. If we pick that up and head north and then west for a mile or so, there's this place called Kynance Cove. It's meant to be really gorgeous. All dramatic rocks and pale sand and green sea water."

"All right," Dave agreed with a great show of reluctance. "As long as it's just one afternoon."

"They say it's very *Famous Five*, you know? That's –"

"Enid Blyton, yeah. Read the books as a kid."

Nicholas was back to glowing happily and walking freely, rather than being hunched and spooked. "This is just the place for an adventure, isn't it? All smugglers and spies, and great long hikes with bars of chocolate in our backpacks."

Dave laughed. They were almost back at the cottage. "I've got the perfect adventure in mind right now."

Nicholas's grin grew broader still. "Does it take place in bed?"

"It does."

"Will there be chocolate?"

"Yeah, I think we can manage some chocolate. You'll need your sustenance, after all."

Nicholas laughed, like a joyous peal of bells. "Then lead the way!"

The following morning Nicholas and Dave ambled into the village to say hello to the woman who acted as housekeeper and caretaker for the cottage when the owners weren't in Cornwall. Along with her mother and daughter, she also ran a small grocery store and news agency. Nicholas and Dave introduced themselves, and she shook their hands with a pleasant smile. "Margaret Widgery. This is my mother Joan, and my daughter Maeve."

The older woman smiled on them benignly from her comfortable chair placed directly in the sun pouring through the front windows. The younger woman said "Hiya" and finished tapping out a message on her smartphone before slipping it away into a pocket and returning to the task of shelving new stock. She had a flower – a white daisy – tucked into her abundant curly red hair.

"I hope you found everything shipshape at the cottage," Margaret was continuing. "It's just as Mrs Brett and her family like it, but you must say if there's anything you want done differently."

"No, it's great," Nicholas said. "I'm sure we'll be very comfortable there."

"I stocked the fridge, of course, but I wasn't sure whether you'd be wanting to eat dinner out, or cook for yourselves …" She paused, and confided with a hint of a blush. "I understand this is your honeymoon, but other than an extra bottle or two of champagne I didn't know –"

"We'll be fine," Nicholas assured her. "We can fend for ourselves, if need be!"

"And may I offer my congratulations, as I should have done before." She shook their hands again, and Dave saw that the daughter was grinning at them, while the grandmother seemed mostly oblivious.

"Thanks," Dave said. He was starting to wonder when he'd encounter someone who *didn't* approve. He wasn't entirely sure how he'd handle it.

"Thank you very much, Mrs Widgery. We're very happy about it, I must say. It's been a *marvellous* few days …"

Before Nicholas could launch into a detailed account of exactly what he was so very happy about, Dave smoothly cut in. "We were wondering if you knew anything about the circle of standing stones near the cottage. Like, the history, maybe."

Margaret looked rather taken aback. "I can't say that I do. It's local stone, as you've probably seen, and they say it dates back well over two thousand years. But more than that – I don't know."

"Any stories, then?" he tried. "Like, what happens if you count the stones? Nicholas said I shouldn't."

"Ah!" Maeve put in rather cheerfully. "If you manage to correctly count the stones, then the Devil pops up and drags you back down to Hell with him."

"And yet," said Dave, "here I am."

"*Why, this is Hell,*" Nicholas muttered, "*nor am I out of it.*"

Margaret looked from one to the other of them – but surely fretting more over the maintenance of their happiness rather than anything real relating to the stones. "It's nothing but tall tales. I'm sure there's nothing at all to worry about."

Then Joan spoke, proving she wasn't so oblivious after all. They all hushed to listen to her quiet voice. "If you see someone up there, sitting on the altar stone …"

"Admiring the view," put in Dave. "It's a great view from up there." Not that they had really looked, now that Dave thought about it. They'd been more concerned with the actual stones.

"I wouldn't go disturbing them, my lad."

"Why's that?" he asked. Though he knew he didn't want to hear the answer.

"Because sometimes it'll be folk having a rest while walking along the coastal path. And sometimes it'll be folk who aren't resting at all."

At which Nicholas was looking decidedly spooked.

"Right," said Dave. "I think that's probably enough hair–raising stories for now."

"Pay it no mind," Margaret urged. "They're just stories."

"Exactly. And we're on our honeymoon. To be honest, I plan to spend most of it safely tucked away in bed." At which Maeve guffawed appreciatively – and Dave abruptly blushed crimson, realising that not only had he managed to set Nicholas's imagination working overtime about the stones but he hadn't avoided the honeymoon–related embarrassment after all. "Oh *God*," he grumbled. "One day I'll learn when to shut up."

At least Nicholas was looking at him fondly, ghosts forgotten for now. "I think that's our cue to leave, taking what little is left of our dignity with us."

"Absolutely."

Margaret kept them long enough to press upon them another business card with her phone numbers, despite them having already found a stack of such cards at the cottage – and to assure them at disconcerting length that she wouldn't be dropping by without phoning first, so they should feel free to *do whatever they liked at any time* without fearing *any surprises*. Soon enough, however, they were out of there.

"I think," said Nicholas, "we should go and do … exactly what they think we're going to go and do …"

"All right," Dave gamely replied. It wasn't as if he could feel any more embarrassed.

"Or … maybe something wickeder still."

Dave grinned at him. "You're on."

They had lunch at a pub in Lizard the next day. It was cold but sunny, so they sat out the front under a canvas umbrella, taking in the view to the south. The land fell away until it reached the southernmost point of mainland Britain. "We should do that, should we?" asked Dave in admittedly lazy tones. "Are we doing the tourist thing?"

"We could wander down there … if I've left you with the necessary energy."

Dave thought for a moment, and chuckled. "There's no right answer to that, is there?"

"No," Nicholas smugly replied.

"Have you done the other points? I mean, north, west, east …"

"No, and I'm not likely to now, am I?"

"Maybe we should do this one anyway. Seeing as we're here."

Nicholas scrunched up his face a bit. "Have you done that in Australia?"

"No … Byron Bay's pretty cool, though. That's the easternmost point. That's worth a visit, anyway. Pete Murray lives there, though he's really a Queenslander."

Nicholas was grinning again. "Will we go on holiday there, do you think?"

"Yeah, maybe." It was Dave's turn to scrunch up his face. "I dunno. Some years, I'm so busy with the tours that just hanging out at home is enough of a holiday."

"I can understand that."

Their conversation might have ambled on forever, if a couple of blokes hadn't come out from the pub with their pints, and sat themselves down at the next table along. And they obviously weren't there for the ploughman's lunch. One was an older man with a white hair and beard, who seemed well–weathered and well–salted. The other was maybe forty or so, with black hair and a devilish glint in his dark eyes made all the more attractive by his narrow sinuous hips.

"Afternoon," the two blokes said in greeting.

"Afternoon," Dave said – and Nicholas responded rather warily, "Good afternoon."

"I heard you young fellows were interested in our stone circle," the older bloke said.

"Well –" said Dave, wondering how to head this off at the pass. Nicholas's face had gone as blank and cold as if the shutters had come down.

"I could tell you some tales, and that's the truth."

"Tell 'em, Bert," the thin one encouraged.

"That really won't be necessary," said Nicholas. He added rather pointedly, "We're on our honeymoon, you see. The two of us – fellows."

Old Bert wasn't put off, but blessed them with a genial smile and actually winked before launching into his story. "My mam told me, from when I was a boy –"

"*Really*," Nicholas continued, "we're far too busy fucking to care about stone circles. And when I say fucking, I mean *each other*."

"Oh aye, I heard that, too," the fellow quite amiably replied, winking again.

Dave couldn't help but let out a laugh. It seemed that Nicholas had been silenced and maybe even a little shamed, so Dave said, "Go on, then. Tell us your tales." And he reached across the table to squeeze Nicholas's hand and then hold it as a gesture of support.

"So, my mam used to tell me, right from when I was a boy, that those stones used to be witches who were dancing around in a circle one May Day, and they was cursed by the local priest for their heathen ways, and turned to stone."

Nicholas was unimpressed. "I thought the stones were over two thousand years old. In which case they're a bit early for priests and heathens."

"*I* heard tell," said the other bloke, "they were maidens of the village who refused the, er … the *attentions* of their local lord and master, and it was him that damned them."

"Right …"

"I heard there are times when the local maidens still dance there," he added with a knowing wink. "Either way, witches or maidens, once a year at midnight every May Day they are freed from the stone for an hour – but still they must dance, though they are weary unto death."

"*And* once a year at midnight," Bert contributed, "when the altar stone hears the church bells ring, it turns over, it turns right the way over."

"Is that also on May Day?" Nicholas asked, in full sceptical mode – though he looked rather paler than usual. "I'm sure no one in the cottage would get any sleep, with all that going on."

They were saved from any further stories when their lunch arrived, and the barkeep chased the two locals back inside with mock threats of never serving them again if they drove away the visitors. Perhaps the barkeep had read Nicholas's discomfort, because he came back to say, "I'm sorry. Bert is mostly harmless, and he can be great company, but Vincent does egg him on rather."

"It's fine," said Dave. "Honestly, it's fine." Then, once they were alone again, he said to Nicholas, "These stories … Don't think about them, if they bother you."

"They don't bother me," Nicholas replied a little remotely. Then after a moment he smiled, and said rather more sincerely, "They don't bother me at all."

Late that night, however, Dave woke in the small hours to find Nicholas standing at the bedroom window, having drawn one of the curtains open, staring pensively up towards where the stone circle must be. "Hey," said Dave, bleary with sleep.

"Hey," Nicholas softly replied. "Sorry. Didn't mean to wake you."

"'S all right …" Dave got up out of bed despite the bed being perfectly warm and comfortable, and went to stand behind Nicholas, wrapped his arms snugly round his narrow waist. He peered over Nicholas's shoulder to see the stones fitfully lit by moonlight. "What's going on up there?"

"Nothing. Nothing, really." Nicholas sighed. "Those are just cloud shadows."

"Not ghosts, then?"

"I think we're going to lose the fine weather."

"All the more reason to stay tucked up safely in bed."

Nicholas huffed a laugh, and then sighed again. "Just what I always wanted … a husband with a one–track mind."

"Come back here, then." Dave took the man's hand and tugged, stepping back towards the bed. Nicholas followed him willingly enough.

It was true that Nicholas generally took the lead when they had sex, but every now and then Dave felt the need to take care of his lover, and this was such a time. He encouraged Nicholas into the bed, lying on his back, and then lay near, leaning over him to kiss him and sooth him with gentle hands until Nicholas finally forgot about the fretting, and thought only of Dave.

Slowly still, Dave knelt up and undressed them one item at a time – first his own t-shirt and then Nicholas's, next his own boxer shorts and then his lover's. His husband's. They were both so very ready, but he didn't rush. He reached for the lube in the bedside cabinet, spread some on his palm and then caressed it onto Nicholas's cock and balls, and his own. Then he lay over the man, matching them up with their legs interleaved, and his hips almost by instinct started an easy rocking motion as he thought about the strong slow surge of the sea.

Nicholas's hands came up to run back over Dave's hair, to shape themselves to his nape and encourage him down for a kiss, and then slowly slowly those hands slid lower down Dave's back, those palms and long cool fingers moulding themselves to every inch of his skin in turn, until at last they were firmly spread on Dave's rear, and Nicholas eventually in desperate need grasped him hard, dug his fingertips in, begged with those midnight-blue eyes …

Dave spun it out for a few moments longer until at last even he felt it was the perfect time, and then he slid a hand down under Nicholas's rear, and they crushed themselves even closer together, each thrusting against the other like mad things – until the end came, and they quaked with it, and clutched at each other, and mouthed kisses over anything of the other they could reach.

Afterwards, as Dave was drifting drowsily, Nicholas said, "I think you should fuck me."

"Mmm?" he managed.

"Not *now*. I mean, sometime. While we're here on our honeymoon."

Dave opened one eye and then the other to peer at his lover in the dark. "If that's really what you want."

"It is. I really think we should."

"All right," he said, though it was more an acknowledgement than an agreement. "Sleep now?" he asked.

"Yes. Sleep now." And Nicholas turned to him, and they snuggled close as they usually did when they slept. But Dave was sure he slipped away first.

nine

The following morning was rainy, so they took the opportunity to laze about, indulge in a full cooked breakfast, and then put their feet up in the front room with a book for Nicholas, the Kindle for Dave, and a large pot of coffee between them. The rain cleared in the early afternoon however, so they decided to walk the coastal path around to Kynance Cove, even if the overcast sky meant they wouldn't be seeing the countryside at its best.

As it was, the place was pretty spectacular. The cove was fairly small, but the rocky outcrops were huge and dramatically shaped, and the sea was running high with milky–turquoise waves dashing white spray. Dave kind of loved the wildness of it. They took a while to watch the waves crashing in, but it wasn't long before the cold wind coming off the sea started biting a bit too deep. Luckily there was a café just inland from the cove, so they headed there for a warming cuppa.

Dave placed their order while Nicholas went to use the facilities. He took the opportunity to ask the guy at the counter if there were any butterflies around at this time of year. The guy consulted with a young woman who happened to be making a delivery, but unfortunately the general consensus seemed to be that there weren't, and certainly not now the weather had finally turned cold. "Thanks anyway, mate," Dave responded.

"What's up?" Nicholas asked once he returned.

"I was just asking about butterflies in the area. I think we're out of luck."

Nicholas smiled at him with a glowing kind of softness. "I know. It's far too cold for them by now, I'm afraid, and not enough flowers to drink from."

"I guess I figured you'd plan any trip like this around butterflies."

The smile grew fonder still. "It's our honeymoon, David," Nicholas said, reaching to hold Dave's hand across the table. "I wasn't thinking of anything but you."

Dave tried to suppress a pleased grin, but didn't succeed very well. He hung onto Nicholas's hand when Nicholas would have withdrawn it. He might be putting his Aussie citizenship at risk for being demonstrative, but Denise had trained him too well over all their years together. She'd had no patience with the restraint of affection beyond what was required by decency.

"But you know," Nicholas continued, his smile turning a bit cheeky, "if you really can't get by without a butterfly sighting, David Taylor – tart for them that you are – we could try at The Eden Project."

"Ah. The place with those big bio domes or whatever they are?"

"That's the one. Just in case I'm not enough for you, and you want a butterfly drinking your nectar, too."

Dave chuckled, and unleashed his best grin. "You know you love that they love me. You don't mind sharing."

Nicholas growled in reply, and his hand tightened possessively around Dave's. "In very rare circumstances … and only with butterflies. Don't you go getting any ideas."

He didn't tease any more, but leaned in against the table edge to murmur, "I'm all yours, Nicholas. I promised you that."

They gazed at each other intensely for a lovely charged moment – but then had to sit back when their coffee and tea were brought to the table. "Sorry to interrupt, guys," the guy said. "Thought you'd like it hot, you know."

Dave guffawed and Nicholas just about hooted with laughter at the hint of innuendo. "Thank you," Nicholas managed. "You're right, we *do* like it hot."

Once the guy headed off again, however, Dave saw that not everyone at the café approved of his and Nicholas's involvement with each other. 'At last!' part of him cried. Someone to challenge them. Someone to face down. Dave needed the practice, he figured, before he went home to Oz and became the subject of teasing and taunts.

There was an older couple sitting at a table nearby; the man was scowling and the woman looked disgusted. They didn't say anything, but they stared in disapproval at Nicholas and Dave as if they expected this would force the two men to quit holding hands so very obviously.

Nicholas hadn't noticed yet, being too busy checking on how his tea was brewing in the teapot. Dave, however, took the opportunity to direct a big uncomplicated beaming smile at the couple. And he leaned towards them a little to confide, "We're on our honeymoon!"

The woman had been about to drink more of her tea, but now she put down the cup as if having lost her taste for it. Nicholas, having finally taken in the situation, lifted Dave's hand and pressed a kiss to the back of it as reward and further provocation. The woman stood up and stalked out, leaving the man to belatedly stand and then grumble a complaint at the café guy on his way out – which was politely shrugged off.

When he came over to clear the couple's table, Dave said, "Sorry. Didn't mean to chase away your customers."

The guy shrugged again. "Who needs them? You two enjoy yourselves. You deserve it."

"If they didn't pay, I'll cover the bill."

"They'd already paid, don't worry about it." And he nodded politely before taking the abandoned tea things away, and leaving them alone.

"My knight in shining armour!" Nicholas murmured, caught between admiration and laughter. "Will you tilt at *all* my dragons … ?"

"Yes," he fervently vowed. "*Yes*. For all my life."

Late that night Dave woke to again find Nicholas standing at the bedroom window staring up at the standing stones. Even taking into account the eerie effect of the moon's cool light, Nicholas appeared pale and spooked. "Hey," said Dave, waking up quite quickly this time. "What are you up to? Come back to bed."

Nicholas glanced at him before returning his gaze to the stone circle. "There were lights up there. I swear I saw lights up there."

Dave frowned, and slowly got out of the bed to go stand beside Nicholas. "What kind of lights?"

"I don't know. Just a couple of dim lights, or maybe a few. Bobbing about."

It took a moment for Dave to focus properly on the stones, and then he stared hard for a while, but there was nothing up there now. "What, like torches, maybe? Or do you say flashlights?"

"We say torches. Could be, but they weren't very bright."

"Fireflies … ?" Dave tried.

Nicholas cast him a look. "*Very* unlikely."

"Well, you're the scientist," Dave responded, a little sharper than he'd have liked, but what could anyone expect from a man woken in the middle of the night? "What do *you* think they were?"

"Will-o'-the-wisps," Nicholas said, just as sharp but with a touch of whimsy.

"Which are … ?"

"Pixies carrying little lights trying to lead you astray."

Dave let that be for a moment. Then he said, "You know, if you just left the curtains closed, they'd protect us. Like the blankets do. We're perfectly safe here in our bedroom. It's like a fort."

"You think this is all in my imagination, don't you?"

"Whether it is or not, as long as you don't go out there and try following the lights over the cliff or whatever, we'll be fine."

"There really were lights, you know. Though I'm assuming people, not pixies."

"Promise me you won't go investigate in the middle of the night."

Nicholas just looked at him rather flatly for a long moment. But eventually he said, "I promise."

"Good. Now, come back to bed, and let me hold you, and maybe we can get some sleep. You'll be perfectly safe."

"I know," said Nicholas, following Dave to the bed with a sigh, as if merely humouring him. Though when Nicholas climbed in after him, he wriggled deep into Dave's arms, and that felt entirely genuine – as did his remark. "I'm always perfectly safe with you."

The next morning after they'd eaten and cleared up breakfast, Dave found Nicholas at the table again poring over their map of Cornwall, measuring things off with a ruler. "What, are you working out distances or something?" Dave asked. "Are we going for a drive today?" He had to admit that taking the Jaguar out for a spin hadn't gotten old yet.

Nicholas looked at him a bit shamefaced for a moment, but then metaphorically girded his loins and announced, "You can draw a line on the map that runs from Lizard Point, through St Michael's Mount, to Gurnard's Head – which looks like a pretty significant promontory on the north coast of Cornwall. And as far as I can make out, the stone circle is right plumb on the line."

Dave let out a sigh. "So, what does that mean?"

"Do you know about ley lines … ?"

"They've been debunked as random coincidence, haven't they?"

Nicholas seemed almost too astonished to be outraged. "I never realised what a sceptic you are! How did you find our waterhole in the Outback? And why on earth does Charlie think you have a Dreamtime connection with the place?"

Dave shrugged. "Dunno. I just think you've got to be careful with this kind of thing. Cos the human imagination is pretty damned powerful, and you can project anything you like on things that don't actually mean anything at all."

"Right," said Nicholas, obviously unimpressed.

"Anyway, if it *is* real – the Dreamtime thing, I mean – then that doesn't necessarily mean I'm gonna feel a connection with other places, too, does it? In fact, maybe it means that I *won't*."

Which Dave thought was an entirely reasonable point, but Nicholas directed a mighty scowl at him, and Dave decided he might as well go get some fresh air before they ended up really arguing. Which he assumed was an activity to be avoided if possible while on honeymoon. "Just heading out for a wander," he announced – and once Nicholas had acknowledged him, he did so.

He didn't go far, but just rambled around in front of the cottage with his hands shoved in his jeans pockets. He didn't go near the cliff edge, as Nicholas was wont to do, but he watched the endlessly changeable sea which was steely–blue today under an overcast sky. Eventually he looked inland, and with a start realised there was a figure sitting on the altar stone in the middle of the stone circle.

For a moment his heart raced as he remembered Joan saying, 'I wouldn't go disturbing them, my lad.' But then the figure waved, and once Dave squinted to focus properly in the diffuse light of the day, he saw that it was actually harmless old Bert.

Dave waved back in a friendly manner, thinking that would be that. But then Bert waved again, somewhat more urgently than might be expected in a greeting between acquaintances, and Dave twigged that Bert wanted him – or them – to go up and talk to him. Dave shrugged, and tried to indicate with another wave, 'Wait there, and I'll be up in a minute.' Well, it looked like Bert wasn't going anywhere for now, so Dave headed back inside.

Nicholas had put the map aside for now, and was on his laptop. "I'm just starting up my blog for the day," he said. "Do you want to go visit the Eden Project? We could take our photo there, with some butterflies maybe. Could be cool."

"Are you writing about us disagreeing?" Though that wouldn't necessarily be such a bad thing. "I suppose that makes it seem all the more real, doesn't it? I mean, no relationship is all plane sailing."

Nicholas sniffed. "It *is* real. But no, I wasn't. Though I may write about us *discussing* the matter. It's not as if either of us is entirely convinced one way or the other, is it?"

Dave grinned at the man, hugely and stupidly relieved. He went over to drop a kiss to the top of Nicholas's dark–haired head, and then said, "You remember old Bert from the other day at the pub? He's up there at the stone circle. I think he wants to say hello."

"Okay. Is he coming down?"

"No, I think he wants us to go up. Is that all right?"

"Yes, of course," said Nicholas. He offered Dave a wry smile. "I promise I won't get spooked."

"Good man," said Dave. And they headed out to meet Bert.

The old fellow beamed at them genially as they reached the stone circle and walked up to the altar stone. He didn't get up from the stone – which was flat and low enough for his booted feet to be firmly on the ground – but he seemed happy enough that they'd come.

"Hello," said Dave. "It's Bert, isn't it? I'm Dave and this is Nicholas."

"Hello," Bert replied. His smile when it turned to Nicholas – as so many people's smiles did – grew sweeter still.

"How are you today?" Dave continued. "Are you taking in the view? It really is a great view from up here." He took the opportunity to finally look at said view himself, which was much the same as the one from their front door, though with added magnificence due to the higher ground. Their cottage looked snug and peaceful from here, tucked away in a rounded dell at the foot of a steep rise.

"Oh aye, I'm well enough," Bert said a bit bashfully, glancing at Nicholas again.

"What do you do around here?" Nicholas asked. "Are you a fisherman?" Which was what Dave would have guessed, too, given Bert's reddened weather–beaten skin.

"Used to be. But my boat – Well, I crew sometimes, for the *Alice May* out of Mullion, during the main season. But my boat, the *Fortune Teller*, is at Cadgwith – and I take tourists out for trips. Cash only, mind. Scenic trips." Bert looked hopefully at Nicholas. "Aye, maybe you'd like to come out, if the weather holds."

Nicholas looked at Dave with a querying brow, but it seemed clear he was interested. "Sure," Dave answered for them both. "If it's safe, you know?"

"Sure," Bert echoed, and his eyes slid away mischievously. "If you can spare the time away from … what you said you were doing here."

Nicholas snorted a laugh. "Sorry about that. I was being horribly obnoxious."

"You're on your honeymoon!" Bert protested. "What else should you be doing?"

"Okay," Dave said, trying to steer the conversation back to smoother waters, "we can probably fit a boat trip into our busy schedule. But only if it's safe. I don't want to be losing Nicholas already when I only just found him, I'm sure you can understand that."

"I know these waters like a landlubber knows his garden. And no one's ever been hurt on board the *Fortune Teller* – aye, nor lost off her, neither."

"Sounds like it could be fun," said Nicholas. "It would give us another perspective on the coastal scenery, at least."

"But I hear there's a lot of shipwrecks off Lizard Point," Dave persisted. "I don't want to add to them, and it's not like we're talking about taking a rowing boat out on a pond, is it?"

Something fired within Bert, though he also seemed confused, even a little uneasy. "Sure, and there's Spanish galleons down there with treasure, and old British frigates! I take people out diving for treasure." He frowned, and then squinted up at Nicholas. "Maybe you'd like to go diving, if the weather holds?"

"No. No, I can't." Nicholas was now looking even edgier than Bert. He appealed to Dave: "I can't. The pressure, you know?" He lifted a hand to his head, though Dave had already understood. Nicholas didn't want to subject his aneurysm to the compression and decompression involved in diving even in shallow waters.

"That's all right," Dave reassured him, though there was a part of him that was sorry to lose the opportunity. "We won't be diving. Is that something you used to do, Nicholas? I haven't even gone snorkelling before, though I wouldn't have minded learning."

"No, I never have – and now I can't."

"It's all right, I understand. We definitely won't be diving," Dave repeated to Bert. "But we'll think about the boat trip, all right? Especially if we have another nice sunny day."

"All right," Bert said, watching Nicholas with both curiosity and anxiety. They were all silent for a long moment, until at last Bert stood up. "It's gonna get blowy soon, but if we have a nice day, Mrs Widgery will know where to find me."

"Thanks, Bert, that's great. Either way, we'll see you soon."

Nicholas remained silent, despite Bert looking at him again, wanting something, even if it was simply acknowledgement.

Then, unexpectedly, Bert said, "You don't come up here at night, do you?"

Dave frowned. "No … No, we don't." He looked at Nicholas, who was likewise frowning, and no doubt remembering staring out their bedroom window at the stones at all hours of the night. "Why?" Dave asked. "Why shouldn't we?"

Bert shrugged, and started sidling off. "There's the cliff and the ground so uneven as can be treacherous and the – the – stones. And well, you don't want to be losing him already, do you?"

"All right," Dave equably agreed. As soon as Bert was out of earshot on his way back to town, Dave grumbled to Nicholas, "What the hell was all that about?"

"I don't know." Nicholas was pale again, though he didn't seem spooked so much as unsettled. "I don't know. Let's head back down and make a pot of tea."

Dave guffawed a little. "That's your answer to everything. You're so English!"

"And you love me for it."

He laughed again, fondly. "Seems that way!"

On the way back down the slope towards the cottage, Nicholas asked a bit edgily, "Are we going to go for a boat trip at least?"

"Not without consulting Margaret Widgery first," Dave said very firmly indeed. "Did you hear that about cash only? Doesn't exactly inspire confidence."

And Nicholas visibly relaxed. "Sometimes," he said – "just sometimes, mind you – I think you're an even better answer than a cup of tea, David Taylor."

Dave grinned at the man, for whether he agreed with it or not, he knew a man's truth when he heard it.

ten

They walked into Lizard the following morning, and headed for the grocery store. Margaret Widgery was there; her mother Joan was sitting in what must be her usual place, and this time Maeve was sitting by her, reading a book, with a white rosebud tucked into her thick red hair. While Dave explained his qualms to Margaret and asked her opinion, Nicholas browsed the postcards.

"Bert knows the sea and the peninsula as well as anyone," Margaret said in response. "He wouldn't take any risks with the tides or the weather. However, he's not an official tour operator. You'd be trusting him as an individual. An acquaintance."

"Do you know if his boat is licensed?"

"Well, I can't say for sure, but I should think so. He takes better care of the *Fortune Teller* than of himself. But he may not be fully insured for passengers, and so on." She caught her lower lip between her teeth, obviously unwilling to either recommend they take the trip or be unfair to Bert.

"I don't care so much about insurance," said Dave, "as about nothing bad happening in the first place."

"Well, there are always risks in taking a boat out to sea. But then there are risks in driving a car along the road – probably more! It becomes about what you're used to." Margaret sighed. "If you'd trust me to drive you to Penzance in my car, say, then you can trust Bert to take you out in his boat for a couple of hours. I suppose that's what it comes down to."

Joan put in, "Bert will bring you safe home again, no need to worry about that. He sails these waters by sun and by moon and by the stars."

"Thank you," Dave said to them both, nodding his appreciation.

"You'll let us know when you go out, though?" Margaret asked. "And let me know once you're safely back."

"Yeah – if we go. I'll have to think about it some more."

Margaret smiled at him. "I'm sure you'll make the right decision."

"And I think I finally have, too," said Nicholas, coming over to the counter with ten or twelve postcards and a pen, which he bought along with stamps. "This will surprise everyone! They'll wonder how we found the time, what with us being on our honeymoon and all."

Dave huffed a laugh, and turned away before he could blush again.

They headed for the same pub to have lunch, and sat outside again, in the sunshine close to the wall so they were out of the wind. There was a wood–burning brazier near them, which helped provide a little warmth and a lot of atmosphere.

Nicholas started writing out his postcards with fluent ease. Apparently he could be just as charming in writing as he was in person. "Take a couple," he encouraged Dave. "I bought plenty. I thought you'd like to send them to Denise and Charlie. They'll be home again by now, won't they?"

"All right," Dave grudgingly agreed, sifting through the remaining pile to pick out the two he found most appealing. However, there was only one pen, so for now he was excused from having to come up with actual words. He hadn't had much practice in the writing of postcards.

The barkeep came out with menus, made a point of welcoming them back, and then took their orders for both drinks and food. As he headed back inside, Dave glimpsed Bert hovering in the shadows just inside the doorway, peering out at them anxiously. When he realised Dave had seen him, Bert withdrew a little further – but it was obvious he was still there. Dave said to Nicholas, "I think Bert wants to come and say hello again."

Nicholas looked around, and waved cheerily – though he turned back to Dave and muttered, "I'm sorry if this bothers you. Rotten timing and all that, given that we just got hitched. But I'm afraid he seems to have taken a bit of a shine to me …"

Dave just stared at Nicholas for a long moment before guffawing. "Are you serious? *Everyone* falls for you, Nicholas. It's a wonder I had any chance at all."

"Oh," said Nicholas, apparently rather nonplussed.

"You just don't get to do anything about it any more. Not with anyone but me. All right?"

"Right," Nicholas agreed, promptly though a little vaguely. "Well, can he come and say hello, at least?"

"Of course." Dave laughed. "It's all right, I'm not the jealous type. But I'm loyal, remember? We're going to be loyal, aren't we?"

Nicholas nodded. "Of course we are. That's what I want, too." And after a moment in which they acknowledged this fundamental agreement, Nicholas turned around again and beckoned for Bert to come and join them.

Bert shambled over and stood there looking a bit shyly at Nicholas. "Hello," he said.

"Hello, Bert," Nicholas replied. "We're still thinking about the boat trip, I'm sorry. I'm sure we'll make up our minds soon, though. It's not like we're here for very long. Hardly more than two weeks, really."

"That's all right," said Bert. Then after a brief pause, he blurted, "But you don't go up to the stone circle at night, do you?"

"No," said Nicholas with a frown. He glanced at Dave before asking, "Why? Why do you keep saying that?"

"It's not safe, it's not good."

Nicholas seemed spooked, but also intrigued. "Why, though? Does something happen up there? Some kind of ceremony, maybe?"

"No, that's not it. That's not it."

"But –"

"Bert! Are you bothering these fellows again?" It was slim, sinuous Vincent who'd come out of the pub to lay a restraining hand on Bert's arm. He seemed just a little too familiar with Bert, as if he knew he could presume. "Remember we got told not to bother these good fellows … ?"

Bert remained silent, but was alternately glancing at Vincent and looking rather imploringly at Nicholas.

"It's all right," said Dave, puzzled by the whole thing. "He's not bothering us."

"Nah, come inside, Bert," Vincent insisted. "You don't believe his tall tales, do you?" he asked Dave and Nicholas even as he tugged at Bert's arm.

"You were telling us tales about the standing stones as well," Nicholas pointed out.

"Fairy stories. Nothing but rubbish."

"Right …" Nicholas sounded sceptical, as well he might. If it was all rubbish, then why did Bert seem so unsettled?

"Come *on*, Bert," said Vincent – and after another tug at his arm, Bert followed Vincent back inside the pub, casting one last longing glance back at Nicholas.

Dave and Nicholas looked at each other. "What the hell?" said Dave, rhetorically.

After a moment, Nicholas ventured, "It's like … there's something Bert isn't saying. Something he's trying to tell us about."

"Something he wants from us?"

"Maybe." Nicholas cast a worried look into the pub. Not that they could see anything inside, given the relative brightness of the day.

"D'you think he's trying to ask for your help?"

Nicholas guffawed, but answered, "Maybe. And maybe Vincent doesn't want him to. But then, why wouldn't Bert ask you? You're the heroic one, David."

Dave smiled despite himself. It was sweet that Nicholas thought so, though Dave himself had to disagree. "No, I'm not."

At least this new topic successfully distracted Nicholas from fretting over Bert and the mystery of the stone circle. "I've told you before: you're the hero of my story," Nicholas insisted.

"And there I was, thinking that you're the hero of mine …"

They gazed at each other with amused fondness – or maybe it was fond amusement – until their lunch arrived.

It had been on Dave's mind that Nicholas had asked Dave to fuck him while they were on their honeymoon, and he hadn't yet done anything about it – so as they made love that afternoon, as they stretched tall and pressed close and kissed wild, Dave let his hand slip down Nicholas's long backbone, his fingertips trailing down each knob and dint, until at last he touched the man somewhere he'd never touched anyone before. Nicholas shuddered in reaction – and, remembering as vividly as if he were touching himself, Dave shivered, too. It was a strange dark glorious kind of intimacy that Nicholas had introduced Dave to. It was certainly more than time to repay the favour.

As Dave teased his fingertips back and forth across that tender pucker of flesh, Nicholas pushed further into Dave's embrace, he moaned and his kisses became ragged with hunger, his thigh slid up higher so that he was more exposed … That all seemed promising. Dave settled in, and slowed his pace to something more deliberate. He rubbed a fingerpad against Nicholas, and pushed gently, feeling the tension and the slight give, remembering that he himself had never really had a problem with this. Not physically. He suspected Nicholas might find the act a little more problematic, but it was

Nicholas who wanted it … It was Nicholas who wanted to be fucked. They'd take it slow, that was all. They'd take it steady.

Dave reached a long arm for the bedside table and the lube.

"No, wait," said Nicholas, his voice husky with need.

Dave left the lube where it was, and met the man's heated gaze. "I was just gonna finger you," he carefully explained. "Nothing too serious. Not yet."

"No – No, I'll –" Nicholas was actually so far gone as to be having trouble with words. He was also, however, adamant. "*I'll* prep myself. Trust me?"

"Yes."

"I'll do that. I want our first time to be full on. I want it to be –" Nicholas groaned gutturally – "*elemental.*"

At which unexpected word Dave groaned, too. And they had a fair go at 'elemental' right then and there, twisting and turning, holding and pinning, to rut hard against each other as if it were the natural order of things. Which Dave supposed it was.

Afterwards, as they lay there sprawled heavily in each other's embrace, even as they were still panting with the exertion, Nicholas commented, "If we can't go up to the standing stones at night, like Bert says, and we can't do it during the day cos anyone might walk past along the coastal path, then it'll have to be first thing in the morning. At dawn. That's appropriate."

Dave frowned over that for a moment, but had to ask, "We'll have to do what at dawn … ?"

Nicholas replied, as if it were perfectly obvious, "You fucking me for the first time."

"What – ?"

The matter–of–fact tones continued despite the outrageous notion. "I want to sacrifice my virginity to you on that altar stone."

Dave was kind of horrified. He shifted his head a little so he could stare at Nicholas. "You can't possibly be serious."

Nicholas blinked, but said "Maybe" in the way that meant he actually was. Then he added, "Aren't you man enough to do that for me?"

"Don't try to out–macho me," Dave grumbled. "You said you felt safe with me! And your father trusts me to take care of you. So you have to let me have a say in things like this. The last thing I want to do is hurt you!"

"Like I said, I'll prep myself. It'll be fine."

Dave let out a sigh. "Yeah, all right, I trust you to do *that*. But outside? On a *rock*? I dunno, Nicholas …"

"We did it outside at the waterhole. Any number of times!"

"That was Australia, out the back of beyond – and on a mattress, mostly. This is England, five minutes from the nearest town – not to mention the fact that it's almost winter!"

Nicholas hauled himself up onto his elbows so he could talk more directly to Dave. "I want it to be – primal. I want to – You said it once. You said you wanted to *feel* it. It hardly counts if it's too easy."

Dave considered the man. Lifted a hand to run a wary, curious finger down that long, determined face. "In the middle of a stone circle …" Dave said rather more quietly. "Don't you think that's just asking for trouble?"

"I thought you didn't believe in all that supernatural stuff."

"Supernatural or not, it seems a bit … risky to me. And did I mention the cold?"

Nicholas was reduced to using his imploring face.

Dave couldn't help but chuckle in response. Nicholas usually got what he wanted, Dave had found. But then even Simon had advised Dave to stand firm – or indeed, run away – when necessary, in his own interests or in Nicholas's. "Let me think about it," Dave eventually conceded. He assumed the answer would have to be no, but maybe he could come up with a half–decent alternative.

Nicholas immediately agreed, "All right," and there was a slight smugness to his smile, despite an attempt at demureness. It was perfectly obvious that Nicholas assumed the answer would end up being yes. Sharing his life with this man might prove to be even more of an adventure than Dave had realised!

During a lull in the cooking that night, Dave caught Nicholas gazing at him curiously. It was so plain that Nicholas had something he wanted to ask that Dave wondered why he couldn't already read the words spilling from those perfectly plump pink lips. Dave laughed, and prompted, "What?"

Nicholas's gaze slid away, and he turned bashful. Which was getting to be a rarity. These days Nicholas was too happy to be shy; confident in all the right ways. Dave took that as the best compliment he'd ever been paid.

"Come on," Dave insisted, unable to prevent himself grinning. "What's going on in that tricksy mind of yours?"

Another pink–cheeked hesitation dragged by until at last Nicholas said, "At lunch? You said that everyone falls for me …"

Dave guffawed. "Well, they do. Everybody *adores* you. Do you honestly not know that?"

"Everyone likes you, too, David."

"It's not the same thing. I get on all right with most people, if I try. And I do try. You don't have to. People just fall for you, no matter what you do."

Nicholas sighed, and grabbed the cloth to wipe down the already clean counter. Eventually he asked, "Why was I alone for so long, then?"

"Were you?" Dave scrunched up his face in thought. "I kinda assumed … I dunno. I guess I assumed you got around a bit. Plenty of boyfriends."

Nicholas seemed to be finding this conversation excruciating, and yet equally seemed determined to see it through. "Well," he said. "I suppose I had my share of … friends with benefits. And … um … acquaintances with temporary privileges. Probably rather too many of the latter," he confessed. And then Nicholas looked at Dave with shocking directness. "But you're only the third guy I've really loved."

"The third? Me and Frank and … ?"

"Oh, a guy at uni. It only lasted a couple of years. Not even that, really. Not properly. I think Frank spoiled me in some ways … It was only ever really friendship, no more than that for him – but he was very … steadfast … in his affection."

"That's not spoiling you. You're entitled to expect steadfast."

Nicholas smiled at him softly. "It's one of the things I love most about you."

"You already know you're only the second person I've ever loved," said Dave in his turn. "It's only been you and Denise for me. And I'm not planning for that to ever change. Not now."

Nicholas nodded vigorously, but his head was down again. Apparently they hadn't quite got to the point of the conversation yet. Dave glanced at the oven timer; they had two minutes, maybe. Though in reality, they had the rest of their lives.

"Hey," said Dave softly, going over there to wrap his arms around Nicholas's waist and push close. To get right in Nicholas's face in the most loving of ways. "Hey, you have to know I reckon I'm the luckiest guy in the whole world, to get lucky with you – when you could have had absolutely *anyone* you ever wanted."

And at last Nicholas lifted his head again, and those deep dark eyes looked clearly into Dave's own. "And you should know, David, that I feel exactly the same way. *Exactly*."

"Do you … ?" Even now he found that hard to believe.

"Yes. You should have more faith in me."

"I have complete faith in you. Not so much in myself, I guess."

"It's the same for me," Nicholas insisted again. "What you just said. It's exactly the same."

"Well, then," said Dave, feeling something within his chest at last relax and warm into utter happiness. A tension he hadn't even known was there was now gone.

"Well, then," Nicholas agreed. And his smile perfectly reflected how Dave felt.

eleven

Dave figured that more research about the boat trip was called for, so he and Nicholas walked around the coastal path to the village of Cadgwith one morning. It took them about two hours, which included time to gaze in awe at the rugged scenery – though they didn't linger anywhere for very long, as the weather was cold and windy. The seas were running high, with waves crashing spectacularly against the rocks and cliffs. Which was all very well to look at, snugly bundled up as they each were in padded coats. This was Dave's first proper coat, and he was certainly beginning to see the merit in it. However, "Right now I'm thinking no about the boat trip, Nicholas."

"I don't think Bert would even consider taking us out on a day like this," Nicholas agreed. The path widened a little, and Nicholas settled into step beside Dave; took his hand in his. And Dave would have hung on no matter what, but on that day he had to admit to himself that he was glad there was no one else about. He still got a bit too self–conscious sometimes about being gay, about having a husband. It was something he knew he had to work on.

Eventually the path took them down a steep hill into the fishing village, and they saw that the weather must be even worse than they'd thought. All the boats were drawn up out of the water onto the stony shore, with a couple apparently battened down for the winter season. Another boat was being hauled up by winch even as they arrived. As luck would have it, the boat turned out to be Bert's *Fortune Teller*. Nicholas and Dave stood out of the way and watched the goings on. Vincent was with Bert, dealing with scuba gear and with his slim figure still snugly encased in a wetsuit, so it seemed he'd gone diving while they were out there. The other boats all appeared to be working fishing boats, and there were the usual sights and strong smells involved in dealing with a catch, including a flock of hovering seagulls. All very vivid and picturesque!

Dave took the opportunity to cast a critical eye over Bert's boat, but he soon had to admit that to a landlubber it looked as sturdy and serviceable as any of the rest of the fleet. Perhaps, if it weren't for the weather …

When Bert was finally free to come over and say hello – casting bashful glances at Nicholas whenever he dared – Dave commented, "There's a storm coming, then?"

Bert looked amiably confused, and for a moment frowned up at the overcast sky. "Um, no … ? Maybe some rain later, and a bit of a blow. Wouldn't call it a storm."

"Oh. I just thought, with you going to all the trouble of hauling the boats up onto the shore …" Dave didn't dignify it with the term 'beach'. He had his standards.

The confusion vanished. "No, we always haul them up here. The sea gets too rough to moor offshore, and the cove's too small to hold even one boat at anchor."

"I see!" It seemed like an awful lot of bother to be hauling boats in and out of the sea, but who was Dave to argue? He noticed that Vincent was nearby, still fiddling with his scuba gear and looking at them a bit edgily. Maybe the man didn't like Bert wasting time on taking tourists out on the water. Maybe he just didn't like Bert paying so much attention to anyone else. "Look, Bert –" Dave began.

"I know. You're still thinking about it."

Dave laughed, and Nicholas offered a shrug with one of his most charming smiles.

"I wouldn't take you out today or tomorrow, it's going to be windy tomorrow, but we're looking at a couple of calm days after that," Bert said. "You just let Mrs Widgery know if you decide."

"Will do. Well –" Dave turned to Nicholas. "Shall we grab some lunch here before we head back?"

"Sure. Thanks, Bert!"

They had offered their farewells and turned away when Bert called after them. "If it rains, Vincent can drive you back home."

"Oh, that's all right," Dave said – for Vincent didn't look very pleased at being volunteered. "It'll hold off, and anyway we'll go cross–country this time. We came the long way round."

"No, go on," Bert insisted. "You really should." After a dramatic pause, he added, "Vincent has a Maserati."

"What?!" Dave exclaimed, thinking that Bert must have got that very wrong. Could he have possibly meant a Mazda … ? But when Dave glanced at Vincent, he received a cool nod of confirmation. A Maserati it was.

Nicholas let out a breath which sounded like '*Wow …*'

"Don't you go getting any ideas if he drives us," Dave cautioned, though quietly so only Nicholas would hear. "You and your thing for chauffeurs," he grumbled.

"Never!" Nicholas took Dave's hand again, and Dave bore it manfully.

"Have your lunch, and come back down in an hour or so," offered Vincent. "I'll run you home before I drop Bert off."

And so they agreed.

The Maserati hardly had the chance to shine in the five minutes of country roads that took them back to the cottage, but Dave and Nicholas were stirred enough to decide on taking the Jaguar out for a spin that afternoon. They headed for Penzance, then drank a takeaway cuppa while considering St Michael's Mount, drove back home again – and then made out in the car until the windows steamed up. The evening played out the way that honeymoons are supposed to …

Late that night Dave woke, and was unsurprised to find that one of the bedroom curtains was open. Nicholas, however, was nowhere to be seen. Dave would have assumed he'd gone to the bathroom, if only Dave didn't have a lingering notion that it had been the noise of the front door quietly closing that had woken him up. Dave cursed under his breath, and hauled himself out of the soft warm bed. He was already dressed in his usual t–shirt and boxer shorts, so he simply grabbed his coat on the way, and made his way outside.

Nicholas was out the front of the cottage, standing on the cliff edge. Dave's heart pounded in fear. From the cottage door, it looked as if Nicholas was *literally* on the edge, and dressed in little more than his dressing gown, too. There was a stiff wind coming in off the sea, so at least that was pushing him back in the right direction – but then Nicholas seemed to be leaning into it as he peered down the cliffs, and what if there was a moment's lull in the wind's resistance, and Nicholas was leaning just a little too far to keep his balance?

Dave walked closer, quietly, not wanting to startle the man, and he veered off at an angle so that he wasn't coming up directly behind him. Once he was about two or three metres distant from Nicholas's left shoulder, he said the man's name in tones that were calm but would carry. "Nicholas. What's up?"

Nicholas didn't seem surprised to find he had company, thank God. He cast Dave a scowl, and said, "I thought I heard something. I'm sure I saw lights."

"Where? At the stone circle?"

"No, on the beach down there."

Dave wasn't quite game enough to get that close to the cliff edge, but he looked to see if he could make out any light that couldn't be explained by natural causes. There was nothing. "Nicholas. No one would bring a boat into that bit of beach with this wind, even in daylight. It would be far too dangerous. They call it a lee shore," he added, drawing on the seamanship he'd learned from Patrick O'Brian. "They'd be driven onto the rocks."

Nicholas was absolutely adamant, of course. His jaw set mulishly.

"There's no other way of getting down there."

"I wasn't imagining it."

"I know. But if they're gone now, we're not going to solve the mystery tonight, are we? Come back inside, Nicholas."

A long moment dragged past while the wind buffeted them. Nicholas seemed to be shaking – though whether from cold or fear, excitement or anger, Dave didn't know.

"Please, Nicholas. Come back to bed with me."

That earned him a reluctant glance, and a protest half–shouted against the wind: "Don't humour me!"

"I wasn't! I'm just frozen through to my marrow, is all." Dave waited until Nicholas glanced at him again, a little more sympathetically this time. "I can't warm up properly without you. Not any more."

Nicholas huffed as if still suspecting that he was being played. But after another long moment he turned away from the cliff edge, and stepped towards the cottage, holding out his hand to invite Dave along with him. The ever–clumsy Nicholas simply turned and stepped away from the edge as confidently as a tightrope walker. And Dave stumbled towards him, took his hand, and hung on.

They didn't talk about it. Nicholas obligingly disrobed and got under the covers and wrapped himself around Dave – not that Nicholas felt much warmer than Dave himself, but with the doona and an extra blanket tucked in around them, they warmed up soon enough.

Despite all of which Nicholas felt tense, as if he wasn't prepared to forgive Dave nor ask for forgiveness himself. Eventually Dave asked, "Why d'you go out there?"

After a brief pause, Nicholas gave a succinct answer: "Curious."

Dave persisted. "What did you think you'd find?"

"Dunno." Nicholas shifted as if shrugging, but seemed to finally relax a little.

"Witches? Maidens? Pixies?"

"Smugglers," was the reply. "This is a *Famous Five* adventure, not a ghost story."

"Oh, *Nicholas*," Dave chided.

Luckily Nicholas saw the funny side of it, for a chuckle bubbled out of him as if he just couldn't help himself – and then Dave laughed under his breath, and soon they were giggling, and wriggling in closer together, and they were warm and happy. Nicholas yawned, and then Dave did, too – and soon they had smiled and snuggled themselves back into a peaceful sleep.

Nicholas wandered out for a breath of fresh air the next morning, while Dave got breakfast ready. Within moments, however, there was a cry of "David!" and then Dave heard Nicholas at the front door again. "David, come out here, will you?" Nicholas called in urgent tones. "Can you leave that? There's something at the stone circle."

Dave had already covered up the food – an Australian habit, apparently, as flies seemed almost non–existent in England – and for good measure he switched off the kettle, though he hadn't known it not to automatically cut off when it was done. "What is it?" he asked as he met Nicholas at the door and then followed him out.

"I don't know yet. I didn't go up."

Dave didn't cast the man a sympathetic look, but instead took his hand as they walked up there.

"See?" said Nicholas almost before they'd even left the cottage behind.

Dave squinted up at the stones. The wind was strong off the sea, so he had to push his hair back to get it out of his eyes. There was something – small. Not a witch nor even a hiker, but something small and yellow or white, apparently tied to one of the stones. The one most directly opposite the sea.

"What –" His mind raced, but didn't come up with any ideas at all.

Nicholas kind of went 'Huh huh' under his breath as if forcing a laugh. "Not a sacrifice!" – as if trying to convince himself.

"Well," Dave reasoned, though perhaps not helping anything, "if it was a sacrifice, it would be on the altar stone, wouldn't it?"

Nicholas just glanced at him, perturbed.

When they got up there, it seemed both relatively harmless and curiously weird. They stood there together still hand in hand, staring a bit gobsmacked at a small bunch of silk flowers bound to one of the stones with a long yellow–gold ribbon. The flowers were yellow and white and –

"Wattle," said Nicholas. "Which is Australia's national flower, isn't it?"

"Yes. And a rose … ?"

"Which is England's." They stared some more in silence before Nicholas observed, "That's you and me. I mean, okay, you wore eucalyptus flowers for the wedding, but otherwise – that's you and me."

"And the gold ribbons –" Dave said a bit faintly, remembering their wedding night. Which no one but Denise and possibly Vittorio could have any idea about. Surely.

"They're not exactly the same kind of ribbons," Nicholas cautiously offered. "Gauze rather than satin."

"It's still kind of creepy," said Dave. He looked about them, but the countryside seemed deserted, the coastal path was empty. "I suppose," he tried, "it could be meant nicely. Kind of … done in our honour. If you see what I mean."

"Could be," Nicholas agreed. "Do you think maybe … Bert?"

Dave laughed. "If it was Bert, he wouldn't have bothered with the wattle. It's you he fell for, Nicholas."

"Oh. Well, I guess that takes us back to creepy instead of nice."

"Maybe that's our imaginations working overtime again," Dave added, diplomatically going for *our* rather than *your*.

"Maybe."

"Well," said Dave at last. The sky was clear, but the wind was cold, and he was dressed in nothing warmer than a light sweater. "Let's have breakfast, anyway. No harm in breakfast, eh?"

"No harm at all," Nicholas agreed. And they walked back down to their snug, safe little cottage, hand still clasping hand.

twelve

Dave woke alone in the small hours again, and saw that the curtains were half open – again. He sighed, and waited in the blissfully comfortable bed for a moment or two, just in case Nicholas had got up for the bathroom. But of course that wasn't it. Eventually Dave sighed once more, and grumbled to himself about broken promises, before climbing out of bed and padding barefoot through to peer out of one of the front windows. Nicholas wasn't out at the cliff edge. Dave went back to the bedroom and looked out to check whether he could see anything happening up at the stone circle. Something seemed a bit off–kilter up there, but there was no Nicholas.

Right.

Dave quickly hauled his jeans on over his nightgear, then his boots, and shrugged on his coat. He picked up his mobile phone and – despite the fact it was a clear moonlit night – he collected the torch from the kitchen on his way out for good measure. It was one of the heftier Maglites.

The wind seemed to have blown itself out at last, and the night–shrouded countryside seemed quiet and still. There was no sign of Nicholas. Dave felt anxiety settle like a stone in his stomach.

He didn't have much of a clue about where to start looking, but he figured the standing stones were as good as anywhere. Also, there had seemed to be something a bit odd about them, though looking up at them now Dave still couldn't quite pin down exactly what or why.

As Dave walked away from the cottage towards the stones, however, he thought he heard something from beyond the cliff edge. A voice, perhaps, shouting out angrily. Certainly something, though he could be projecting human qualities onto a bird's cry or a wave's crash.

He headed towards the cliff, not too proud to lower himself to hands and knees once he got close, and cautiously shifted forward until he could at last poke his head over the edge just far enough to peer down.

One thing was immediately apparent, and that was the boat moored just off the little beach at the foot of the cliff, a boat that was of much the same shape and type as Bert's *Fortune Teller* and the other small fishing boats they'd seen at Cadgwith. There was also a dinghy drawn up on the sand. The beach seemed empty otherwise –

Until a figure stepped out from the cliff's foot, collected something from the dinghy, and cradling it in both arms took it back to where he'd come from – not breaking his stride even once as he neared the cliff, so Dave thought there must be some kind of cave down there, even if not an extensive one.

There was the sound of a voice again, and then an answering one. So that was at least two people involved. And Dave couldn't help but fear that Nicholas had got himself mixed up in this somehow. He had no idea what was going on – though it was hard not to think smugglers – but if Nicholas was down there, then Dave had to go fetch him back. That was all.

How Dave was supposed to get down there himself was another matter. He didn't have a boat, and it would take too long to try tracking down Bert in the middle of the night; Dave had no idea where he lived. The cliff was obviously impossible for him to scale; the rock face wasn't even, but all the ragged folds and edges ran vertically.

Dave scrambled backwards, got up to his feet, and looked around. There was nothing. No clues or hints as to how to proceed.

But his attention was again caught by the stone circle. There had been something odd, he remembered … That would have to do as a starting place.

Dave headed up to the circle as fast as he could – and was gobsmacked for a moment by what he found.

The altar stone in the centre of the circle had been shifted by about half its width towards the sea, to reveal a hole in the ground with crudely–hewn stone steps leading down into the dark. Dave stared at it for a long moment, then switched on the torch to see what else he could make out.

There wasn't much. The steps – some man–made and some raw rock – continued down into what otherwise looked to be a natural fissure. There was also a rope running along just overhead, which reached the entrance and then doubled back. Dave's first guess was that this was to provide handholds, but changed his mind when he realised the rope seemed to follow its own route directly down into the darkness at a steep angle, while the steps twisted around out of sight just two or three metres down.

Right. If there was a cave behind the beach at the foot of the cliff, then Dave had to assume this led down to it. And if Nicholas was nowhere else to be found, then Dave figured he must have come up to the stone circle to investigate – despite Bert's warnings, or maybe because of them – and ended up stumbling into whoever had brought that boat to the beach. And he must be down there now.

Dave took a breath. Had another look around him at the surrounding countryside – which still seemed deserted. And then took the first step down into the tunnel.

At irregular intervals the steps and the bits of pathway – such as they were – rejoined the rope in its more direct descent. Dave made his way down through the cliff as quickly as he dared, hanging onto the rope where he could and otherwise keeping at least one hand in contact with solid rock. At some stage, however, the rope running over his head began to move. He'd had hold of it at the time, and was startled enough to almost lose his balance, but steadied himself with both hands against the rough rock walls.

The fissure wound down through the cliff almost vertically. At two points so far, the makeshift stairs had been replaced by wooden ladders fastened to the rock in a ramshackle way.

Dave continued on, no longer using the rope which kept moving fairly steadily. Eventually a package hanging off the loose length of rope loomed into the circle of light cast by his torch. It was startling, but by then he'd half–expected it, so he simply crouched down where he was until the package trundled on past him. It seemed to be a canvas bag holding a clumsy collection of objects that rattled together. Whether that meant smuggling or not, Dave didn't care very much at this point.

What he cared about was Nicholas.

Eventually the fissure opened out into a larger cave, and Dave followed a foot–worn path further down until at last he could hear the waves surging onto the beach, and under it a murmur of voices. He switched off the torch, and carefully made his way nearer. He figured it was worth his while remaining hidden until he could work out what was going on, so Dave crept towards the cave mouth staying low behind a ridge of rocks.

At last he could look out past the far edge – and the first thing his gaze swooped upon was Nicholas. Dave's heart thudded in relief as he took in the sight of his husband, alive, in one piece and apparently unhurt. He was sitting on a rock next to Bert. They both seemed anxious, and concerned for each other, and Nicholas's posture seemed a little cowed. Dave suddenly felt swamped with hatred for whoever had bowed Nicholas's head and rounded his shoulders.

The apparent object of his hatred strode into view. It was Vincent, of course – looking rather spectacular, even Dave had to admit, with his wetsuit peeled off down to the waist and his chest still alluringly wet. The man was gesturing angrily and demanding, "Well, what d'you think we're gonna do now?!"

Bert gazed back at Vincent with pathetic sorrow, but Nicholas set his jaw. "You're going to let us part ways without any more threats," Nicholas said. "That's what's going to happen."

Vincent sneered. "What, so you can run off to the cops and spoil my game?"

"I don't even know what your game is." Nicholas turned to consider his companion again. "I get the impression that Bert wants out, but if you let him go – if you quit using him and there are no other victims, then I actually don't care very much about you carrying on smuggling or whatever."

"Don't try to con a con."

"I'm not." Nicholas's posture suddenly straightened and his tones and demeanour became more aristocratic than Dave had ever witnessed in him before. "I'm sure *my* class cares as little as *yours* does for legal restraints on self–interest."

Vincent's devilish eyes seemed to fire with fellow feeling. "You understand, then," he said, stepping forward to plead his case. "There's this old frigate down there. Not burdened with treasure, but enough to set a man up nicely. Finders keepers: that's fair, isn't it?"

"It seems fair to me," Nicholas said with convincing sincerity. "But the less you tell me, the less I know, if push ever comes to shove."

Vincent was too stirred up to quit, though. "It's three months in the clink and a five–grand fine just for not *telling* them about a treasure trove. Not to mention having to hand it over."

Nicholas dared to raise a sceptical brow. "They pay you for it, don't they?"

"Yeah, but as little as they can get away with. Anyway: finders keepers. Fair's fair."

"Agreed," Nicholas crisply replied. Then he turned to Bert, and said in a quietly encouraging voice, "Was there something you wanted to say to Vincent, Bert?"

A silence dragged while Bert gathered himself. He seemed oddly bashful for such a potentially dangerous situation. Eventually he said – to Nicholas – "I'm sorry. I'm sorry."

"Don't be. You must always ask your friends for help when you need it. Now, what did you want to say to Vincent … ?"

Bert finally brought himself to echo Nicholas's words in a small voice: "I want out, Vincent."

"Oh, *do* you?" Vincent retorted. "*Why?*"

"Don't wanna go to jail – nor pay such a fine!"

"Chances are we'll get away with this. No one knew until you got this fellow curious." Vincent gestured angrily at Nicholas.

"Feels as if everyone knows – and no one likes me for it – and it frets me – when all I want to worry about is fishing and taking a few people out on boat trips, and making them happy. I'm a simple man, Vincent. The simplest."

"Oh come on, Bert," Vincent said in increasing frustration. "It's almost winter, anyway. It's not like we'll have more than another one or two trips this season."

Bert sat there quite woebegone.

"See this season out with me, and then we take a break. We don't have to decide about next season – not for months yet."

Bert was upset, though he managed to repeat quite firmly, "I want out."

"And the cash?"

"Don't want it. Haven't used it." He gazed up at Vincent as if eager to please. "You can have it all back, Vincent, if you want. Well, almost all," he added with scrupulous honesty. "You know I had the *Teller*'s engine overhauled … You can have the rest!"

Vincent growled in annoyance, and turned away. "Where am I gonna find another boat? Who's gonna crew for me?"

Nicholas replied rather crisply, "I'm sure that's your own concern, and not Bert's. Not any more. Although," Nicholas added with a glint of humour, "if you try walking around town dressed like that I'm sure you'll find a man soon enough who's willing to do your bidding."

A finger stabbed through the air towards Nicholas. "Don't you *dare* count me in with your queer lot!"

"Well," Nicholas retorted, "quit taking advantage of a good man's affections, and I won't!"

A silence seemed to indicate that Vincent acknowledged the hits and was stuck for further arguments. Bert had apparently achieved his goal. Which would have felt better if it wasn't partly due to Vincent not wanting to be seen as Bert's partner in life as well as crime.

More importantly than that, though, Dave felt so bloody proud of Nicholas for having handled this with such firm tact. The only question that remained was how they could all withdraw from the current situation with good grace.

"Well," Nicholas eventually continued, apparently thinking along the same lines. "What usually happens now? Vincent follows his treasure up to the surface, and drives away in his suspiciously expensive car –"

Vincent swung back around to glare at him. Nicholas didn't even falter. Dave just loved him to the stars and back.

"– and Bert, you take the boat back to Cadgwith, do you?"

"I spend the night out on the boat, and go ashore at dawn."

"Oh … because of the boat having to be hauled out of the sea? There isn't anyone to do that for you at this time of night?"

"That's right. It's not that there isn't, but it draws attention we don't want."

Nicholas nodded. "All right. So there's no reason why we three can't go our own separate ways, then, is there? You two just do as you usually do, and I'll climb up to the stones with Vincent and then head back to the cottage."

Bert gasped a little, and grasped Nicholas's closest hand. "No, you'd better come with me on the boat."

"If I don't show up until morning, David will be worried. He might already be wondering where I am. I can't do that to him – and you don't want him raising hell trying to find me."

Vincent complained in surly tones, "I'm not letting Bert go off, on his own or with you. Chances are you'd dock at Mullion, and turn me in."

"If I give you my word –" Nicholas began.

"I know how much that's worth, from my lot or from yours."

"Don't trust him," Bert said to Nicholas – in a mutter that carried perfectly well to Vincent and to Dave where he was still in hiding. "Don't go with him. Not on your own."

Vincent crossed his arms and stared at the other two forbiddingly.

"There's no need to fear a 'convenient accident' happening to your friend, Bert. If he fell down a ladder and died, you'd know just where to bring the cops, and who to blame. You'd be a witness, wouldn't you?"

"So you might hit me on the head, too," said Bert.

"Oh, for fuck's sake … This is a sweet game, but not sweet enough to risk two killings for."

Bert, however, refused to be reassured; he clung to Nicholas's hand as if genuinely afraid for his life. Dave figured that it was time, finally, for him to make his presence known.

When Dave stepped forward into the light cast by the lanterns, Vincent was shocked rigid but too cool to want to show it, and Bert was confounded into doing little more than gaping and blinking at Dave – though he quickly pulled his hand away from Nicholas's as if badly caught out – while Nicholas burst into the brightest happiest grin. He instinctively started to stand up and come to Dave, but Vincent gestured menacingly to indicate that Nicholas should remain where he was, so Nicholas sank back down beside Bert. He still looked blissfully happy, though.

"What the hell – ?" said Vincent.

"Thought another witness might be useful," said Dave. "It takes murder right off the agenda."

"How long – ?"

"Long enough to know what's going on. I'm with Nicholas. If you let Bert out of your arrangement, we'll turn a blind eye to your treasure hunting. But people will know how to get in touch with us once we've left Cornwall, and we'd be happy to dob you in if you do the wrong thing by Bert. I think we're all in agreement on that, aren't we?"

There were nods all round – reluctant from Vincent, eager from Bert, and accompanied by a glowing grin from Nicholas.

"So now I think you let Nicholas accompany Bert on his boat. He can have the boat trip he wanted after all. And I'll climb back up through the cliff with you, Vincent, and see you on your way. We'll all be guarantors for the others, see? I'll drive down to Cadgwith, and wait for Bert and Nicholas to come in at dawn. If you're worried, Vincent, you'll have plenty of time to hide any evidence. Though what you'd do with the Maserati, I have no clue."

Silence.

"All right?" asked Dave.

Bert was beaming by now, and he shyly slipped his hand back into Nicholas's. "Yes," he answered.

"Yes," Nicholas said, still watching Dave, though also squeezing Bert's hand in reassurance.

After a long moment, Vincent nodded again.

And so that's what they did.

Dave had few qualms about trusting Bert with Nicholas. The man seemed more besotted than ever, so surely would protect Nicholas with all but his life, and his shambolic helplessness seemed to fall away once he was dealing with his boat. Dave handed Nicholas into the dinghy, exchanging a significant look with his husband – and on a sudden flash of inspiration, he gave Nicholas his mobile phone, muttering, "Tell you why later; just take it." Nicholas did so with a nod, slipping it into his coat pocket. Then Dave helped Bert push the dinghy off into the sea. "See you in Cadgwith," Dave said for them all to hear, exuding nothing but confidence.

"See you, mate," Nicholas replied. His quiet use of the Aussie vernacular felt infinitely reassuring.

Bert nodded at Dave, solemnly conveying his sense of responsibility, before bending to take up the oars and adding a strong stroke to Dave's shove and the sea's flow.

It wasn't that Dave didn't have any misgivings over Nicholas's safety, but Dave knew that he himself was in more danger in Vincent's company, and he was content that it be so. In fact, he wouldn't have had it any other way.

Dave watched as Bert reached the *Fortune Teller*, fixed the dinghy, helped Nicholas aboard, and then weighed anchor. Nicholas waved cheerfully at Dave, before turning to talk with Bert. Soon the boat had quietly puttered away from land and then out of sight in a southerly direction.

"All right," Dave said brusquely to Vincent once he was sure that Nicholas was out of harm's way. "What do you need to do now?"

"Nothing," was the equally brusque reply. "Climb back up to the land above."

"Let's go, then."

With mocking politeness, Vincent swept his hand out to invite Dave to lead the way.

"No, thanks," Dave said, figuring that neither option was entirely safe, but keeping Vincent in his line of sight had to give Dave the advantage. "After you."

They both carried torches, and they were both fit, so the climb was a steady one, with Dave maintaining a careful couple of metres between himself and Vincent, and keeping a wary eye out for any 'accidentally' falling objects.

Soon they were making their way up the last few steps and clambering onto the level grass within the stone circle. They hadn't spoken since they'd left the beach. Dave watched Vincent unhook the bag of treasure from the top loop of rope – but then when Vincent bent to shift the huge altar stone back into place, the man said, "Turn around. I don't want you seeing the trick of this."

Dave backed away a few steps in order to keep his distance, and then obligingly turned. He stared out across the sea, and despite his intention to pay careful attention to Vincent, found himself searching … After a moment Dave spotted a faint light and then a slight wake foaming pale behind a dark shape. Bert and Nicholas would be fine, Dave figured. No doubt Bert would regale Nicholas with seafaring tales for what remained of the night, while Nicholas waxed poetical about butterflies. Perhaps it was his imagination, but Dave could have sworn he heard a faint ring of laughter from over the water.

If he did, however, it was lost a moment later in a grinding noise and then a solid thump, which indicated that the stones had been returned to their rightful places. Dave turned back around. "Well. I doubt we'll be seeing each other again. But just in case," he continued, "you should know I recorded most of that on my mobile – and the phone is now out of harm's way with Nicholas. I'm really not interested in using that unless we hear you're taking advantage of Bert again, though."

It was a bluff, but Vincent fell for it. The man looked absolutely ropeable, and muttered a curse through gritted teeth.

"I'd wish you well –" Dave offered brightly.

"Save your breath," Vincent advised. And, slinging his bag of ill–gotten gains over one shoulder, he turned and strode off in the direction of the main road. No doubt the Maserati was tucked safely away somewhere nearby. Dave couldn't wish the Maserati itself ill, so instead of an accident in these narrow Cornish lanes Dave imagined a story involving Customs or the Tax

Office or whatever, and anonymous tips from concerned citizens … Surely Vincent wouldn't avoid justice for too much longer.

"And good riddance to you," Dave said under his breath. Once he was sure he was alone again, he turned and made his way down to the cottage.

Most of the night was already past, and there was only about two hours left until dawn by Dave's reckoning. He took a few moments to dress properly, and make up a thermos of strong coffee. And then he drove the Jaguar over to Cadgwith, and quietly parked down near the stony beach. After turning off the ignition, Dave got out and looked around, listening carefully. All was still and peaceful. He didn't seem to have disturbed anyone. No one came to ask difficult questions about his business there.

Dave sighed, and got back into the car, left his window cracked open for the sake of fresh air, and drank a cup of coffee. After half an hour or so he got out to wander back and forth on the asphalt in order to stretch his legs. There was no sign of Vincent having changed his mind and coming back to do away with witnesses. All in all, things seemed to be going their way.

Dave tried not to think too much, or let his imagination gear up into overdrive. He'd have brought the Kindle and read, but didn't want to attract attention with a light, nor end up too distracted to notice anything untoward. Instead Dave simply waited for the safe return of his husband. He let his mind dwell on memories of Nicholas, right from that first moment of clumsiness at the Brisbane airport when Nicholas had quite literally fallen at Dave's feet. Dave hadn't appreciated it at the time, but in retrospect he treasured Nicholas's bright smile as he lay there on the floor, already admiring what he saw. And Nicholas had been so confident in his pursuit of Dave – not due to arrogance, or having tickets on himself, Dave certainly knew that now if it had ever been in doubt. Instead Nicholas's happy confidence had been a gift from his family, so rich in unconditional love as they were.

After a while, Dave returned to the car and drank more coffee while standing there beside it. He considered the beautiful little cove in the moonlight, and lulled his anxieties with the sound of the waves crashing rhythmically in, one after the other and another one after that, endlessly.

Nicholas would be fine. No doubt he was enjoying himself out there on the sea on this magical night, with the dangers past and Bert adoring him. No doubt Bert was enjoying himself, too, and Dave had to hope that the man's crush on Nicholas would at least serve him better in the long run than his attraction to Vincent – though it was doomed to come to nothing. Nicholas Goring was a married man now, after all.

The time passed and Dave waited, sitting in the car again for a while, and then walking about. He drank more coffee, though he doubted he would have fallen asleep in any case. He took the time to examine the winch system and figure it out, thinking that he might have to be the one to use it once Bert's boat returned.

At last the horizon beyond the cove began lightening, and the world grew hushed with even the waves crashing calmly before running back down through the stones with a gentle sigh. The horizon glowed, and Dave's surroundings took on a cool grey clarity.

A light appeared in a cottage window behind him – he saw it in the rear view mirror – and then another. People were stirring.

And then just as the sun peeked up out of the sea and colour fled back into things, Dave heard a boat puttering near.

Someone had come down to the boats and seemed to be preparing to go out fishing for the day. "Morning," the man said to Dave, not questioning his presence.

"Morning," Dave replied.

The fisherman turned his head as the puttering drew closer. Dave thought he himself could recognise the boat by its engine noise, but he knew for sure when the man asked easily, "Old Bert been out for the night again?"

"Yes. He took my – my partner out for a trip."

"Oh, aye," the man agreed, apparently still finding nothing much to surprise him in all this.

Dave relaxed a little. And then the *Fortune Teller* appeared beyond the headland, and Dave could just make out Nicholas's tall slim figure beside Bert at the wheel – and Nicholas waved, which made Dave's heart thud in relief and gratitude for his safety – and Dave went to help the fisherman with the winch, silently singing a stirring song, for everything was working out just perfectly.

Bert slung a ladder over the side of the boat where it sat perched high, and then handed Nicholas over. Nicholas climbed down carefully, apparently still feeling his sea legs – and a moment later he was wound tight around Dave, deep in Dave's arms. They weren't too proud to cling to each other. "You're all right," Nicholas babbled. "David, you're all right."

"Of course I am," Dave stoutly replied. "You weren't fretting, were you?" Which was more for the benefit of the fisherman than anything else. The deal was that they wouldn't blow Vincent's cover, after all.

"Of course I was. And I bet you were fretting, too!"

"It's true, I was. But here you are, and you're all right."

They clung for a few moments longer, and then Bert was there beside them, watching Nicholas with a yearning undiminished. Nicholas played his part – detaching himself from Dave, shaking Bert's hand and saying, "Thank you, that was marvellous." He turned to Dave to add, "It was so great seeing the coast at night! So dramatic! And it was moonlit so we could see church spires and another standing stone and a ruined castle …"

Dave grinned at him. "I'm glad you enjoyed yourself." He shook Bert's hand, too, and thanked him, then said to his husband, "Shall we head home? I think there's some coffee left in the thermos, if you want it."

"I do," Nicholas replied with surprising intensity. "I *do* want it."

"Oh," managed Dave, hoping his blush didn't show up in the early morning light. And then he and Nicholas nodded farewell to Bert and the other fisherman – and headed for the Jaguar in a kind of controlled dash.

"It's their honeymoon," Bert could be heard indulgently explaining in their wake.

Nicholas rested his hand hot on Dave's thigh during the interminable few minutes it took to drive back to the cottage. They didn't speak.

As soon as they were inside, they were kissing mouthily damply while shedding clothes – their own and each other's – haphazardly stumbling their way through to the bedroom.

"Nicholas –" Dave managed as they tumbled into the room. Nicholas pushed at him so Dave fell back onto the dishevelled bed – then Nicholas was on hands and knees across him, reaching a long arm for the bedside drawer and the lube. "Nicholas –"

"Hush. It's all right," was the confident reply.

Dave helped Nicholas wriggle out of his boxer shorts – and then they were naked but for one of Dave's socks which he just couldn't be arsed about. Dave moaned a little in fear and anticipation as Nicholas squeezed out a generous dollop of the lube. It wasn't that this act had ever really hurt Dave, but then there was an edge to Nicholas's passion that morning that felt a little alarming. "Nicholas …" Dave groaned, his thighs already opening for the man.

But Nicholas hushed him again, straddled Dave's hips, knelt up tall – *and reached behind himself to apply the lube.*

"Oh God," Dave muttered. "Oh God."

And then Nicholas was positioning himself – lowering himself – and it was happening, it was happening, they were both gasping with the need, with the pain – for Nicholas was as tight as any virgin – but Dave knew Nicholas wanted it that way, he *wanted it* just exactly so, Dave could tell – so he clasped a hand to each of Nicholas's hips and tugged him down further – they both cried out in a joyous agony – Nicholas grasped at Dave's forearms to keep himself upright – and Nicholas let his weight sink further, he forced himself down even as Dave pushed himself up – and it was extraordinary, Dave had forgotten how extraordinary it was to thrust himself inside another human being – it was so hot, so hard, so glorious. Soon he was buried deep within Nicholas and Nicholas had given himself utterly over, his head slumping forward and his hands now loosening from where they'd marked Dave's skin, his arms now stretching wide as his head lifted and fell back – and Dave bucked up *hard*, brought his feet in close and took his weight on them – then as he lowered his hips again Nicholas carefully rose – and they crashed back together – and then they were *fucking* they were *fucking* – and it was raw and awesome and elemental, and Nicholas's deeply resounding groans meant that this was what he wanted, this was exactly what he'd wanted – and Dave took heart from that – he took courage and boldness from it – and after a few magnificent thrusts Dave grasped Nicholas's hips harder still, hauled him down and then pushed himself up so he was sitting with legs loosely crossed and Nicholas in his lap – Nicholas took Dave's head in both hands and devoured his mouth and cheeks with bites and licks and kisses – which was gorgeous but Dave couldn't thrust like that and he wanted to *thrust*, so Dave at last tumbled Nicholas over onto his back, those long legs aslant over Dave's back – and he thrust in hard, he thrust himself into Nicholas even while their right hands met on Nicholas's cock, and they tugged at him *hard* and *rough* until moments later he spilled with a guttural yell that reverberated all the way through Dave's cock and balls and they were both coming so damned forceful that sensation was a rush of dark ocean, and for a moment the stars blinked out.

"Oh God," said Dave.

"God, I *needed* that," said Nicholas. He seemed utterly happy, sprawled back in abandon – not in pain at all. Still, of course Dave had to check as best as he could that Nicholas was okay.

Dave hauled himself out of the bed and went to find a clean face washer, ran it under the hot water, and wrung it out. Returning to the bedroom, he knelt by Nicholas, grasped a hip and gently rolled him over. Nicholas went with a happy whoop, which on the whole indicated he was fine. Still, Dave took his responsibilities towards this man very seriously. He carefully wiped Nicholas clean, and looked for blood, but there was none, not even a speck.

"I'm fine," said Nicholas, still sounding blissfully happy.

"I'm glad," said Dave, rather inadequately though with a full heart. He tossed the face washer aside and collapsed to lie beside his love.

Nicholas rolled over again and they drew each other into a mutual hug. "I really needed that, David," Nicholas repeated, quietly this time. "Thank you."

"My pleasure," Dave replied quite honestly.

"Thank you for *not* being gentle with me," Nicholas persisted.

"Idiot," Dave grumbled. "Love you."

Nicholas sighed quite contentedly and wriggled in closer. "Love you, too." After a while they slept.

thirteen

"Your admirer is wanting to see you again," Dave announced. It was the following morning, and Dave had been taking the kitchen rubbish and recycling out to the bins when he'd seen Bert sitting on the altar stone up at the stone circle, waving eagerly, just as he'd done once before.

"Oh good," Nicholas brightly replied. Then he cast a half–apologetic look at Dave. "Well, you know … I wanted to be sure he's all right before we leave."

"Of course," Dave stoutly agreed, rather than making a pointed remark about the romance inherent in Nicholas and Bert's moonlit boat trip. "Look," he said, "are you really okay with letting Vincent go free? Can we live with that?"

"Can you?"

Dave shrugged. "Part of me wants to turn him in. But mostly, I guess I just want to be sure that Bert is all right."

"Me, too." Nicholas seemed to feel a mix of relief and guilt, but there didn't seem to be much they could do about that.

"Hopefully no one else gets hurt between now and whenever justice finally catches up with Vincent."

Which rather deflated poor Nicholas. "True."

Dave changed the subject. "Looks like there's more of those gold ribbons tied around the stones, too."

"Oh! So it was Bert, then? Even the flowers?"

Dave shrugged. "Guess so. Falling in love will make a man do unexpected things."

Nicholas just grinned at him so very happily.

By the time they got up to the stone circle, they found not only Bert up there but Maeve as well – and even old Joan, who apparently wasn't as sedentary as they'd assumed. The three locals appeared to be in a celebratory mood.

"All right, Bert?" asked Nicholas.

"All right, Nicholas," the old man replied with his cheeks pinker than ever and his shy smile almost as sweet as Nicholas's own.

"We wanted to thank you," said Maeve, with an expansive gesture that took in the nine gold ribbons each fluttering in the morning breeze. It was a cool day, but quite sunny, and rather delightfully fresh.

"Ah, then it was you the other day," Dave said. "And the flowers, too." He should have guessed already. Maeve had a white and gold frangipani bloom in her hair today – silk, of course, but beautiful nevertheless.

"Yes," she answered. Then as Maeve read their looks of relief, her face fell. "Oh … That kind of creeped you out, didn't it?"

"We just didn't know who," Nicholas explained.

"Or what or why," Dave added.

"It was nice, though."

Maeve grimaced in remorse at Joan. "It was meant to be a handfasting ceremony … without the actual hands. A gesture of support, yeah? We'd heard that some people have been a bit … disapproving."

Nicholas was now gazing at Maeve with great interest. "A handfasting ceremony … ?"

"Completely redundant, I know," she continued with a shrug. "You're already married."

"We had a civil partnership ceremony," Nicholas explained. "And we'll be registering our relationship in Queensland once we get there. But it's not marriage." Nicholas turned to Dave. "I figure that if we can ever get properly married – here or in Australia – we'll do that, too. Won't we?"

Dave had to laugh. "Is that *another* proposal?"

"Yes," Nicholas immediately replied, grinning like the most delightful of idiots.

"Then of course we will."

Nicholas soon turned a bit sheepish, however. "It's not that the civil partnership doesn't count. And I wouldn't put you through another whole big thing with everyone there, I promise. But the more anniversaries the merrier, right?"

Despite the fact there were other people there hanging on their every word, Dave took the time to think about that – and then leaned in close to quietly ask Nicholas, "It's not that you don't think I'm committed, right? I mean, you don't *need* an extra set of vows to be sure of me, do you?"

"Not in the slightest," Nicholas averred, lightly yet honestly. "I am *totally* sure of you."

"Okay, good. Is it about the visa thing, then? Proving our relationship to them?”

Nicholas paled, and metaphorically took a step back. “They’ll think I’m trying too hard, won’t they?”

Dave smiled, and lifted a hand, shaped it to that beautiful face. “They’ll know you mean every single word.” And when Nicholas seemed reassured, Dave straightened up again, then glanced at Maeve, wondering if this were even possible. He asked Nicholas – in his regular voice, so they’d all hear – “Nicholas Goring, you wanna get handfasted with me?”

“Yes,” was the instant response, with the most gorgeous smile for Dave. “Yes, I do.” Then Nicholas turned to Maeve. “If we can …”

Maeve turned to Joan. “Gran can do that for you. Can’t you, Gran?”

The old woman nodded quite happily. Bert was beaming blissfully and yearning wistfully all at once. Nicholas looked like he was floating on air.

“Let’s get that done, then,” said Dave.

Which was how they found themselves later that afternoon, the five of them reconvened at the stone circle along with Margaret, who had closed the store for an hour so that she could attend as well. Joan was standing by the tallest stone nearest the sea, with Nicholas and Dave facing each other before her, and with Bert at Nicholas’s shoulder and Maeve at Dave’s as their witnesses. Nicholas had insisted it was Dave’s turn to choose the clothes, so they were both in proper shirts, knitted sweaters and blue jeans. And Dave decided that the circle of standing stones was a pretty special place after all, and certainly more significant than the Disraeli Room, but mainly because he and Nicholas and their new friends were making it so.

Joan recited some words in Celtic or Cornish or whatever in a soothing cadence, and then Maeve read out parts of a poem by Thomas Hardy about him meeting his first wife Emma in Cornwall, which Maeve had adapted to fit the two men. Dave had never been much into poetry, but a few lines of it stayed with him: *‘The man whom I did love so, and who loyally loved me.’* But, really, who cared about getting the genders right when the truth of the feelings transcended all?

‘And shall he and I not go there once again now winter’s nigh,
And the sweet things said that October say anew there by and by?’

Maeve finished there, and then Margaret gave them each a silk flower to hold – wattle for Dave and a rose for Nicholas. As they each clasped their flower to the other's wrist, Joan bound a gold ribbon around them, from one forearm to the other. Then she led them in their renewed vows.

"I David Taylor take thee Nicholas Goring to my wedded husband for a lifetime, till death us depart, and thereto I plight thee my troth."

Dave loved the quaint old words, so much more poetic than the formal vows for the civil partnership ceremony had been and definitely far more like a proper wedding.

Nicholas vowed the same, and not as tongue–stumblingly as Dave had done. Then they kissed with an intensity that even now felt new to them both. And it was done and done again, and no man nor woman would ever put them asunder. And if they even tried, Dave found himself fiercely thinking as he gazed into Nicholas's deep dark blue eyes – they'd have to deal with the stroppiest bloody Australian who'd ever lived.

corroboree

fourteen

Nicholas hated goodbyes so they were barely spending forty–eight hours in Buckinghamshire. They drove back from Cornwall in time for dinner on one day, and were flying out from Heathrow in the evening two days later. Nicholas had even asked that no one but the usual family members should be there – though of course he was inundated with phone calls, texts and emails from the others – so on that first night Dave and Nicholas sat down to eat with Richard, Robert and Penelope, Robin and Isabelle. Everyone was perfectly jovial, in an apparent effort to save Nicholas or themselves too much grief. Only Robin every now and then betrayed the tragedy of it all when the act cracked apart and his sorrow showed through. Young Robin's heart was breaking for the first time.

No matter how ready the general joviality, however, there could be no pretending that Nicholas wasn't leaving. Mrs Gilchrist was cooking every last one of Nicholas's favourite meals. Nicholas's room was strangely empty because Simon had organised the packing of the books, clothes and other belongings that they couldn't take with them on the plane; it was currently all on a container ship somewhere on its way to Australia.

Asked to fetch Nicholas for dinner on that first night, Dave had finally tracked him down in the garage, sitting curled up in the passenger seat of the MGB V8 roadster quietly talking with Frank Brambell who sat beside him with both hands on the wheel of the car he'd never drive again. Dave had crept away as best he could across the gravel driveway, and announced he'd failed in his hunt. Luckily for Mrs Gilchrist's peace of mind, however – not to mention Dave's – Nicholas showed up barely five minutes later.

On the full day Dave and Nicholas were in Buckinghamshire, the family held an afternoon tea to which were invited all the people associated with the estate and most of those living in the nearby village. The women – led by Frank's wife Agate – presented Nicholas and Dave with a handmade queen–sized wedding quilt which included their names and the date of their civil partnership ceremony in embroidery, and a colourful kaleidoscope of butterflies in patchwork. Dave was too astonished and Nicholas too moved to say very much in response, but Agate filled the silence with a humorous description of the women's quilting bees, such a creative shambles as they worked to a tight deadline, and then Richard thanked them very properly indeed on behalf of his beloved son and son–in–law.

Seeing their full names stitched into the quilt set Dave to thinking. He snuck away once the afternoon tea was done, and did some research on Nicholas's laptop. When a rather drained–looking Nicholas joined him in the half hour before dinner, Dave was all set. "I was thinking about our names," Dave announced.

"Yes?" Nicholas prompted, collapsing back onto his bed as if it were quite possible he would never move again.

"Our last names, I mean. We've each kept our own."

"Yes …" Nicholas agreed, somewhat warily.

"I figure you don't want to be Nicholas Taylor, and – no offence – I don't want to be Dave Goring."

Nicholas propped himself up on his elbows and considered Dave with narrowed eyes while he waited to hear where this was going.

"So I was thinking maybe we could do the double–barrel thing, and both be Goring Taylor."

Silence.

Dave suddenly lost his nerve. "If you think – I mean – Well, I don't want to presume –"

"You're perfectly entitled," Nicholas said, cutting him off.

"Really?"

"*Yes.*"

"We'd have to do it by Deed Poll, but –"

"No, that would be –"

"I figured you'd like it if we –"

"Awesome. That would be awesome."

"Cos we're a family now, yeah? Even if it's just the two of us."

Nicholas stared at him, *glowing* with intensity.

"If you think your family wouldn't mind, that is."

"David, they're your family, too, now." Nicholas got up, still looking drawn and pale but also charged with purpose. "He'll say yes, of course. He wouldn't even expect me to ask permission. But I want to talk to my father about it. All right?"

"Of course," Dave agreed, absolutely fine with that.

"I think he'll love it as much as I do," Nicholas continued, not moving from where he stood.

"Go on, then. If it's a good thing –"

"It's a good thing," Nicholas confirmed.

"Then go and make him happy. He deserves it."

Nicholas set off, but stopped by Dave to press a kiss to his temple. "Love you," he said.

"I know."

"I love you so very much – David Goring Taylor."

Dave grinned at him. "Exactly."

Nicholas hadn't returned by dinnertime, so Dave wandered downstairs on his own. Which was fine, of course.

Except that he happened to see Nicholas coming out of the study, and quietly closing the door behind him. And it was perfectly obvious that Nicholas was in tears.

Dave's first instinct was to see what he could do to make things better. But then he figured that actually he might just make it all worse. And anyway, Nicholas had his head down and was making for the downstairs bathroom. He wasn't looking for Dave, so maybe Dave should just let things be. He'd always known that this parting would break Nicholas's heart as well.

What with the Earl himself being absent as well, dinner was served fifteen minutes late. But when Richard appeared, he seemed fine, he seemed as robust as ever – and he shook Dave's hand very firmly, before announcing this latest news to the family with great pride.

Nicholas, still rather pale, held Dave's hand under the table and nevertheless had a good stab at eating the lamb shank casserole Mrs Gilchrist had prepared. And really, Dave had to assume that everything was going to be all right. They were all going to be all right. He just knew it.

Thanks to Richard, they flew first class to Australia, which of course was well–meant – but Dave found the unexpected surroundings a bit unnerving and Nicholas was subdued in any case. They did little more than hold hands and watch movies – manually synchronising them on both their screens – until at last an exhausted Nicholas fell asleep. Dave kept holding his hand, and just sat there, waiting through the hours of darkness. He hadn't travelled enough to have got the knack of sleeping on planes.

Dave didn't get much rest during the stopover at Singapore, either. Nicholas was still really out of it, so Dave just sat on the floor in the departure lounge with his back propped against a wall, and Nicholas lay himself out along the carpet with his head pillowed on Dave's thigh. He didn't fall asleep again, but Dave stroked his hair gently and Nicholas seemed to find that soothing.

Finally they touched down in Brisbane, a few minutes ahead of schedule. Denise came to meet them at the airport, and drove them home. She'd already stocked the fridge for them and made up the bed, so once she was sure they were sorted, she left them to it. The two of them still didn't talk much. After putting on a load of washing, Dave drove them into the city, and they wandered the botanic gardens for a while, just as they'd done when first they met.

It was a warm day, with an infinite blue sky. Nicholas seemed to draw strength from the sunlight as he tilted his face towards it, letting the sun find him under the brim of his Bluegrass Green Akubra. Dave watched him fondly, until at last Nicholas smiled at him – a little wobbly perhaps, but genuinely. They smiled at each other, and held hands – went home and made love, and slept. And on the next day they woke, and their new life together in Australia truly began.

Charlie came to visit them one day, bursting with a surprise. "You've been invited to a corroboree, mate."

Dave stared at him, flabbergasted. "You've been talking with the elders about the waterhole … ?"

"Yeah. And they're cautious. They're not giving much away. But they invited you – and Nicholas – to attend this corroboree. And more than that, Davey, they want *you* to actually take part in it."

"God!" Dave blurted. He hadn't really expected Charlie would get very far with his crazy notion that maybe this white fella should become the custodian of the old Dreamtime site Dave and Nicholas had rediscovered.

"Don't get too excited, mate, it's pretty much a show put on for the tourists. It's the real thing, but it's not the important stuff. There'll be no sacred boards, no secrets shared – you know?"

"Yeah, of course … but that's really cool!"

Nicholas was watching all this with a glowing gaze. He'd always found it perfectly right and obvious that Dave could have a Dreamtime connection with the land, even if he was the wrong race, the wrong colour. But that was love for you. Nicholas would always see the best in him, even if Dave didn't quite believe it of himself.

"It's a small step, baby steps," Charlie continued. "You white fellas get impatient with us, I know, but at least they're showing an interest. At least they're doing you this courtesy."

"Not just a courtesy," Dave said, from the depths of his heart. "It's an honour. I feel really honoured."

Charlie grinned at him, and looked beautifully smug. "You'll be right, mate. You'll be just fine."

Before that could happen, however, Nicholas experienced his first Christmas in summer. He seemed rather bemused by it all. In the heat, Nicholas had taken to wearing a light t–shirt and long canvas shorts, staying in the shade as much as possible and wearing his Akubra when he couldn't, and of course drinking plenty of water with ice and lime juice. Dave was surprised to find that the Brisbane climate didn't seem to worry him too much. When Dave quizzed him about it, all Nicholas did was shrug and say, "I'm happy." Once he added, "I'm where I belong," and Dave didn't feel the need to ask so often after that.

On Christmas Day, Dave and Nicholas had Denise, Vittorio and Zoe over for lunch. They cooked steak, sausages and onions on the barbecue out on the veranda, while Zoe crawled around on the grass and wrestled happily with the colourful plush butterfly toys Nicholas had gifted her. Lunch was served with salads and damper, and then finished off with an Ice Cream Christmas Pudding from an old recipe that Dave's mum used to make.

Afterwards, Zoe napped while the adults stretched out on deck chairs and talked a little or maybe drifted off into a snooze. Eventually Denise announced that she and Vittorio were still trying to decide on a name for the baby they were expecting.

"Well, what have you got so far?" asked Dave.

"Nothing that both of us like."

"I like Zoe," he said musingly.

"Already taken."

They all laughed at her retort, before Dave explained, "I meant that was a good choice, so how did you settle on that?"

"Oh, long story," Denise brushed him off with.

"Really not relevant," Vittorio added.

Then Denise asked, "Nicholas, what are your favourite names?"

Nicholas blinked and returned her look for a long silent moment, obviously puzzled. "I've never really thought about it," he eventually answered. "I've always known I'm never going to have a child of my own to name."

"But if you did," Denise persisted, "what would it be?"

"Well …" He took his time with that, but the others let him. They each sipped at their beer or water–and–juice, and contemplated the backyard – which Dave felt was in pretty good shape despite having been abandoned for the entire spring season and more.

"Well," Nicholas eventually said, "I always thought Bethan is a nice name for a girl, and maybe … Aidan for a boy?"

"Cool," said Denise. "Dave, will those do?"

"Fine by me," he replied.

"There we go, then!" she said, exchanging a satisfied grin with Vittorio. "Problem solved."

"What?!" cried Nicholas.

"We figured that if you and Dave are the godparents – irreligious, mind you – then you might as well do the hard work for us."

Nicholas had been rendered speechless. Stranger things had happened, but not often. Dave went over to him, and knelt beside his chair, took him into a massive hug. They held onto each other tight. And Dave murmured into Nicholas's ear, "You're where you belong, husband. You're where you belong."

In the evening Dave and Nicholas drove down to the nearest beach on the Gold Coast, and wandered along the white sands in their Akubras as the sun westered. They drew a few odd looks for walking hand–in–hand, but no one bothered them.

After a long silence broken by nothing but the crash of the waves surging ashore, Nicholas said, half–surprised and half–contented, "I could get used to this."

"It's pretty good," Dave agreed.

Nicholas smiled at him with utter fondness. "It's idyllic." His hand was hot on Dave's thigh all the way back home to Brisbane.

The Greatest and Best Mystery in the World
To be honest, there are times when we're still trying to work each other out.

But my father says that even after we've been together for fifty years, David will still be able to surprise me. And not only is he probably right, I suspect that it's actually a good thing.

Because it seems to me … the feeling that you already know all there is to know about another person, that you might even know them better than they know themselves – that's the death knell of a relationship, isn't it?

I can't imagine that ever happening for us.

David Goring Taylor, I want to spend the rest of my life trying to figure you out.

The corroboree was held in the new year on a *bora* ground long used for these public ceremonies, a clearing in the bush where there were large circles inscribed in the earth, with a pathway linking them together. The people started to gather together in the crisp morning air, both participants and audience, somehow mingling a sense of respect with a growing sense of excitement. Dave figured that was all right, though, as even Charlie was grinning with enthusiasm at the prospect of the rituals they'd enact that evening.

In fact, Charlie was again bursting with a surprise. "Nicholas my man, you've been invited to dance, too."

"Really?" Nicholas asked, gaping a little.

"With the women folk," Charlie added mischievously – though somehow they knew he was deadly serious. He looked from one to the other of their gobsmacked faces, and admitted, "They're taking the mick, of course. But the invitation's real enough. If you want to accept it."

A pause lengthened, and Dave scrambled for the right words to politely refuse on Nicholas's behalf.

Except that once Nicholas had found his voice, he said quite firmly, "Of course I will."

"You will … ?!" Dave asked, flabbergasted yet again.

"Of course," said Nicholas. "Whatever you need, David. Whatever we need to do to make this work out for you."

"But I couldn't ask …" He didn't think he could bear Nicholas being made fun of.

Nicholas drew himself up tall, and sniffed disdainfully. "I shall probably get to wear a better hat than you, so don't go thinking I'll be at all unhappy."

Dave barely had time to grasp his husband's hand in gratitude and exchange a look swelling with love before they were separated and each taken away to learn the songs and dances.

They were only taking part in the final song of the ceremony, but even so it took quite an effort to learn the unfamiliar words, and then the rhythm, and the melody, and finally the accompanying dance. There were three young Aboriginals who were learning along with Dave, however, and it didn't seem to come much more naturally to them than him. Charlie was participating, too, but he seemed to think it proper to leave Dave to his own devices. At least this song was the time at which all the disparate groups converged, so any mistakes Dave made would be hidden within the whole, just one person amidst about fifty others. But he was determined not to make any mistakes if he could possibly help it. He and Nicholas were the only white fellas participating in the corroboree, of course, and Dave felt all the force of the compliment again and again throughout the long day.

They each kept to their own group for a dinner which combined a Western barbecue with traditional bush tucker, and then it was time to dress. Dave was allowed to wear khaki shorts, though he felt that was cheating a little as the Aboriginal men wore a loincloth type of arrangement. He was barefoot, and adorned with all the same decorations, however, including strings of feathers hung around his neck and bound around his waist, and body paint. Not to mention an impressive conical head–dress also painted with significant designs.

At last it was time to begin. Even the audience had been taught a song, because the corroboree started with everyone joining in a general round of singing. Then the formal rituals began, with small groups of men and women each taking turns to enact a short Dreamtime story. Dave watched from the sidelines with the rest of the male participants, every now and then permitted to take part in providing percussion using the song sticks. He kept an eye out for Nicholas in the distant women's group, of course, but didn't manage to see him. Nicholas was probably trying to be discreet.

Finally they were ready for the big finale. A long pile of dry grass was set alight as the men moved into the *bora* ground, with the flames alternately illuminating and making silhouettes of the dancers' bodies. The audience were almost as enthralled by the drama of it as the dancers themselves were.

The men did their thing, with Dave at last discovering that maybe he had a feel for this after all. How awesome to be a part – no matter how temporarily – of this extraordinary community! The rhythm of the song keened through his blood and the melody grounded him as he stamped his feet and jumped, creating a pattern of tracks in the sandy ground.

Then the men pulled back again though they kept singing quietly with their thighs quivering – and at last there came the women, singing in counterpoint to the men, and approaching the *bora* ground in a united group with stamping feet and a sashaying dance step. And there was Nicholas, his beloved Nicholas, amongst them, singing right along with them, and dancing in his adorably clumsy way with every now and then a bit of show–tune pizzazz sneaking in there. Like Dave he was barefoot and wearing shorts, and like the women he had old dugs painted on his bare chest along with other patterns, and a broad swirling brim of feathers and leaves round his head like an earthly halo. He was all man, despite all or because of it. And Dave had never seen anything so beautiful, so wonderful before, and he faltered in his song, and just stood there for a moment, beaming at Nicholas – who glanced at him with delight kicking up the corner of his mouth – before Charlie nudged Dave, and he fell back into the rhythm and the joy of it with a full heart.

When the women retreated in their turn from the ground, then both groups renewed their songs and began approaching each other – Dave was one of the men approaching the women, dancing his way towards Nicholas, who was dancing towards him, too. And they met halfway, the men and the women, Nicholas and Dave – and it was probably horribly inappropriate but in that moment the love was everything, the love was all, so as the dance ended Dave took Nicholas's hands in his and he leaned in to press a kiss to his husband's mouth, and the whole camp erupted in laughter and a glorious cheer.

About Julie Bozza

Ordinary people are extraordinary. We can all aspire to decency, generosity, respect, honesty – and the power of love (all kinds of love!) can help us grow into our best selves.

I write stories about 'ordinary' people finding their answers in themselves and each other. I write about friends and lovers, and the families we create for ourselves. I explore the depth and the meaning, the fun and the possibilities, in 'everyday' experiences and relationships. I believe that embodying these things is how we can live our lives more fully.

Creative works help us each find our own clarity and our own joy. Readers bring their hearts and souls to reading, just as authors bring their hearts and souls to writing – and together we make a whole.

I read books, lots of books, and watch films. I admire art, and love theatre and music. I try to be an awesome partner, sister, daughter, friend. I live an engaged and examined life. And I strive to write as honestly as I can.

I have lived in two countries – England and Australia – which has helped widen my perspective, and I have travelled as well. I love learning, and have completed courses in all kinds of things. My careers have been in Human Resources, and in eLearning and training, so there has always been a focus on my fellow human beings and on understanding, conveying, sharing information.

Knitting gives me some down time and the chance to craft something with my hands. Coffee gives me stimulation and a certain street cred. My favourite colour has segued from pure blue to dark purple, and seems to be segueing again to marine blues.

I think John Keats is the best person who has ever lived.

And that's me! Julie Bozza. Quirky. Queer. Sincere.

If you want to know more, please do come find me at juliebozza.com and libra-tiger.com.

Titles by Julie Bozza

The Butterfly Hunter Trilogy:
    Butterfly Hunter
    Of Dreams and Ceremonies
    Like Leaves to a Tree
    The Thousand Smiles of Nicholas Goring

Albert J. Sterne:
    The Definitive Albert J. Sterne
    Albert J. Sterne: Future Bright, Past Imperfect

Novels and Novellas:
    The Apothecary's Garden
    The Fine Point of His Soul
    Homosapien … a fantasy about pro wrestling
    Mitch Rebecki Gets a Life
    A Night with the Knight of the Burning Pestle
    A Threefold Cord
    The 'True Love' Solution
    The Valley of the Shadow of Death

Stories and Anthologies:
    Call to Arms
    A Certain Persuasion
    An English Heaven
    No Holds Bard
    A Pride of Poppies